Ugly Angels

Brien Feathers

Brien Feathers

Copyright © 2023 by Brien Feathers

All rights reserved.

No portion of this book may be reproduced in any form without written permission from the publisher or author, except as permitted by U.S. copyright law.

Any references to historical events, real people, or real places are used fictitiously. Other names, characters, places and events are products of the author's imagination, and any resemblances to actual events or places or persons, living or dead, is entirely coincidental.

Cover designed by JV ARTS.

Contents

Content Warning

This book contains strong language, graphic violence, and intimate situations.
Reader discretion is advised.

One

Nocturne

They said the children of the night came from the faerie but that wasn't true. They had always been here, hidden. Unlike the lycans and their faerie masters, vampires were creations of the Maker. At the beginning of the twenty-first century, at the brink of the Third Great War, when time used to exist, humanity had opened a portal to a dying world that the Maker in all his wisdom had locked away. On that day, the old calendar stopped and the era of the Bloodline War began. Since then, cruelty became the mark of all creatures, of this world or otherwise.

Vitali had called all the hostesses of his dens to the walk and Kara stood among them, keeping her head low. It was daylight out there, and being closest to the edge she could see it. The hostesses lined the walls of the tunnel on each side while Vitali dragged an iron crate with Celeste crying inside. She'd stolen from Vitali. He was going to walk her in the sun and make a show of it—he always did.

"This is what happens when you fuck with scavengers," Star whispered, and pinched Kara's side. He meant well. She let him be.

Celeste had been their roommate, and Reef, her scavenger boyfriend, would come over often talking about the Longdark and how they could make it to Lyon during the three-day solar eclipse. In the end though, scavengers being scavengers, he'd convinced Celeste to steal *krystallis* from Vitali, and blood-fiends being blood-fiends, they'd smoked it all. They'd never see the Longdark because Reef was already dead. Vitali tore his head off.

Silver through the heart, beheading, and sunlight were the three ways a vampire died—sunlight being the most brutal.

"Kara!" Celeste screamed, her hand outstretched through the bars as Vitali tossed the crate outside.

A long chain rattled after it, the lead wrapped around Vitali's wrist. Kara covered her ears and a phantom music started in her head so she wouldn't hear the awful cry. No one was allowed to look away, and she had to watch as Vitali pulled the crate back in. Celeste was burning and they threw a bucket of water on her, which steamed, then Vitali threw her out again.

He did this three more times, until there were only charred bones and a pile of wet ash in the crate. The redhead with freckles on her chest as if she sunbathed at the beach, the girl who'd been a kindergarten teacher before the war and had taught Kara to read human letters was gone. Celeste hadn't been her human name, but when she had a real name she'd lived in an apartment on the third floor, had two cats—Athos and D'Artagnan—and she'd been in love with her neighbor in 3B. She used to reminisce about these things when she was high.

"Steal from me, and I'll walk you in the sun," Vitali said, to which all the hostesses nodded. It hadn't been the first show and it wouldn't be the last.

Vitali was seven feet tall, wore a genuine leather jacket with spikes on the shoulders, and a thick gold chain with a snarling bear pendant around his neck. He had a greasy ponytail and chest hair spilled out through the unbuttoned collar of his silk shirt with flower patterns. Not visible at that moment, but he had belly hair—Kara had seen him without his clothes on, as had all the hostesses of his dens.

Before they began the five mile descent back to Nocturne, Kara flicked a look up at the pristine blue sky beyond and thought she saw the most peculiar thing ever—an airplane hanging from the cotton puffs of clouds. She blinked and shook her head, but the shape in the sky remained.

"Come on, bitch." Star grabbed her elbow. "Let's get going unless you mean to walk out in the sun."

"Do you see that?" Kara pointed at the airplane.

"Careful!" He yanked her back. "You're going to blister your arm."

The shape in the sky had disappeared when she looked again. A trick of the mind, Kara assumed. She looped her arm around Star's and let him lead her down into the dark tunnel. Star, with long straight hair that he dyed blue and an immaculate manicure that matched his locks, and Eshe with puffy curls and flawless bronze skin, were Kara's two other roommates. Eshe came to Kara's other side and took her arm as well.

Star and Eshe were fullbloods, vampires who used to be human but were turned, as opposed to purebloods like Vitali and his goons who had two vampire parents and were born that way. Both purebloods and fullbloods had nocturnal sight, but not Kara—she was a halfblood. In vampire terms, a halfblood was someone whose mother was turned while carrying an unborn child. Conceived human but born a vampire—halfblood. They were rare and their sight was crap in the dark. No one could see in the pitch black, but a vampire's eyes captured light better and saw sharper in the dim.

The walk to Nocturne was armed to the teeth and rigged to death with iron bars and checkpoints every fifty yards. The antennae of the landmines buried under gravel and debris glowed only in the blacklight Vitali carried. The hostesses followed him precisely so as not to trigger them. Iron was lethal to the faerie and the descent to the pit of Nocturne was a throat of a leviathan with jagged iron teeth. Although it'd been over a century since the faerie crossed the Atlantic Ocean, the Bloods—Vitali's clan—didn't play with security.

During the five mile walk in high heels, the hostesses gossiped about Celeste, saying how she had it coming. Perhaps they were only saying it because Vitali could hear them, but Kara bit her lower lip till it bled so she wouldn't speak out of order. She couldn't love and didn't feel sympathy, but rage was a familiar emotion inherited from her father. She tried her best to keep it suppressed but sometimes it had a way of surfacing. Kara felt for the iron bangles on her wrists that Star called 'fugly'—fucken ugly—and it doused her anger like a splash of cold water.

Nocturne was a two-hundred-mile-long catacomb of dark corridors, dust, and bones. Time was lost in the city of the undead, one continuous night lasting an eternity. Kara thought she'd been here for three decades, but it could easily be four, or even ten. She didn't know what year it was, no one did, and they thought it was autumn when the tunnels flooded and the power breakers went out. Fall was a wet season and the water seeped in through the limestone walls when it rained above.

The catacomb was made of rooms as much as it was of winding tunnels, and in the one Kara kept her things in she lay on Celeste's mat spread upon a mound of earth along the wall. The graffiti was left behind by the humans, and one next to Celeste's bed was of a clown holding a scythe. In the corner where Star and Eshe were erecting a house of cards on a stone slab was a depiction of a man in a bowler hat. One eye painted black, he was holding a knife. Underneath him, it said, 'A Clockwork Orange'.

Humans and vampires used to have many languages and many letters but only one remained now, the one Celeste had taught Kara to read in. But certain words such as 'day' had lost their meaning because that measured twenty-four hours, and no one knew how long an hour was. 'Day' in Nocturne meant it was light above but didn't signify a length of time.

Star and Eshe built a house out of cards, stacking it higher and higher till it collapsed, and they would start over again. More than once, they'd used the entire deck of cards—a perfect house.

Krystallis, the lifeblood of Nocturne that kept law and order, was crystallized synthetic blood diced with diamorphine and methamphetamine—fancy words with a lot of letters, terms Celeste used to know. It should have been just crystallized blood, but for decades Vitali had been dirtying the supply with long words. Ideas like this got Celeste walked in the sun. It was best not to repeat them, even in one's mind. Because ideas had a way of taking hold, spreading like the plague, and infecting others till everyone died of it. Kara shook her head.

Everyone had a tick, a thing they repeatedly did when they smoked *krystallis* and didn't sleep. Celeste used to construct music in her head and her fingers would twitch playing an imaginary piano—that was her tick. Star and Eshe stacked cards, that was their tick. Taking out the things from her fugly satchel and staring at them was Kara's tick. So she got up to do that. It hadn't been a purposeful thing but a compulsion that comforted her.

One by one, Kara took out the things from her fugly satchel, lined them in a row on the dirt, and looked at them in the candlelight. She arranged them in the order she favored them.

One, a glass heart with a photo of a couple inside it: a man with a white shirt and black suspenders hugging a woman in a white dress and a crown of woven flowers. They were looking at each other while the sun set behind them.

Two, a heart locket with a keyhole but she didn't have the key.

Three, a heart-shaped red box tapered at the edges. It had a dirty stuffed bear inside, crouched as if it was hiding.

Four, another locket, and although shaped like a heart, it wasn't red. It was clear and had dried flowers trapped inside.

Five, a wooden keychain, a square with a heart cut out from it. 'She stole my heart' it said about the missing piece.

Six, a porcelain heart that said, 'Be Happy'.

Seven, a pink knitted heart, a tiny pillow that fitted on her palm.

She also had a handful of sticks that glowed when snapped in the middle, flares, candlesticks, a copper lighter that made a knocking sound when she flicked it open, a glass pipe that cost fifty *dinne,* a plastic bag of *krystallis* with a sad, single shard left in it, a shoe with a broken heel that she meant to get fixed, and the heel of said shoe.

Kara dropped her last shard into the glass pipe and flicked her lighter open, but the wheel turned without a spark. The flint was gone. That would be five *dinne* at the tattoo parlor. Besides shoddy inkwork, they also sold pipes, lighters, flints, and fuel.

Seeing as how her lighter didn't work, Kara held her pipe over a candle flame and rolled the thick glass bowl side to side, letting the shard heat and melt into a red liquid. As soon as Kara took a hit, Star came over.

"Give it, bitch." He held out his hand.

An unspoken rule of Nocturne, no one shared their pipes or bags, but Star had a habit of asking Kara because she had a habit of handing it to him.

"Is that all?" He looked at the empty pipe after he cleaned off the last of it. "Eshe, do you have any left?"

Eshe checked her garter, then shook her head.

"For the Maker's sake," Star hissed. "Get ready then, bitches, off to work." He said 'bitch' in a way someone might say 'darling' and both Kara and Eshe got up to comply. Not to him, but to the fact that they needed to earn *dinne.*

Krystallis cost a thousand *dinne* per 3.5 gram baggie. The blood may be synthetic and dirtied with long words, but without blood, vampires turned pale.

Starved vampires drank each other, and the cannibalism poisoned their minds, turning them feral—pales. They didn't wear clothes or respond to names. They didn't collect trinkets or need candlelight. Pales inhabited the fringes of the catacombs and were always silvered on sight. Vitali may be cruel but he kept order and his tight rein was the reason Nocturne had survived when so many other nests had failed.

Lyon, the nest Celeste wanted to run off to, was already pale—had been before Kara came to Nocturne. She hadn't said so to her friend because it was over three hundred miles away and not a distance a vampire could cross in a single night, which was why Celeste and Reef had been waiting for the Longdark. But Kara would have no reasonable explanation for her knowledge. She sighed because she'd let her friend have hope of escape. She sighed because withholding the truth was akin to lying, wasn't it?

I don't have friends anyway, she told herself. Diamorphine was what mattered. It kept the nightmares at bay. So she got ready with the girls, washing in a bucket of rainwater because she was a hostess after all, and in Nocturne, the dens were open all 'day'.

Airplane

Lucien had been digging into the armrest, testing his nails against the lacquer of the polished wooden surface. He'd never been away from home and anxiety was a strange thing, like a boiling pot left unattended. Andre and Dedreh, the two others in the cabin with him, were Francis's men and he didn't know if they could be trusted.

"You all right, Lucien?" Andre asked and when Lucien lifted his gaze the fullblood was staring at him.

"It's fine." Lucien leaned back into his chair and crossed his legs. "I'm just not used to flying. Tell me about Vitali."

Andre shrugged. "Apollo's oldest son, the Blood leader. That's all I know."

"He has a younger brother, Sedric," added Dedreh, blowing red mist, exhaling *krystallis.* Andre and Dedreh were seated together and across the aisle from Lucien. "The brothers run Nocturne, home to ten thousand the last we checked. It's probably more now. They accept strays."

This, Lucien already knew, and it wasn't helpful. Sending only two fullbloods with Lucien in negotiation with the Bloods, Silverfox's sentiment had been that Francis was trying to get him silvered. He had been livid.

"Should there be trouble, you *will* foresee it, yeah?" Andre asked. He had green eyes that grew brighter when narrowed, and blond hair the tone of his skin. Cut so close to the scalp, he looked bald.

"Only a few seconds, Andre," answered Lucien.

"Few seconds lead is a lifetime of advantage in a fight," Andre said. He looked honest, and 'looked' was the operative word.

Dedreh had earth-toned skin, bright red braids, and none of them had prior dealings with Bloods. From what Lucien understood, the Bloods were physically larger, possessed marble skin like armor, tough to penetrate even with silver, and superior strength in their enraged state.

It dinged in the cabin and a seatbelt sign came on along with Sean's voice through the speakers. "This is your captain speaking. I hope your flight was enjoyable although we have no flight attendants. We're beginning our descent over Sector Five ruins, so buckle your seatbelts, and should we catch fae fire and explode, well, then we'll all be cooked. Should we all die, I hope to see you in heaven. If not, I'll put in a good word with the Maker."

Lucien closed his eyes and clutched the armrest he'd been scratching as the plane vibrated from the steep drop. Resurgence pilots had a habit of diving rather than gently descending. They'd been trained that way because the faerie needed to breathe and below twenty-five thousand feet was where they flew. Landing or taking off was when the planes were most vulnerable and Resurgence pilots hauled ass through it.

This wasn't a fighter jet but a passenger plane, and every bolt in the frame rattled and the cabin light flickered as the plane plummeted. Lucien felt as if he would levitate had the seatbelt not been dragging him down with the plane. He wanted to vomit but there was a certain assurance in seeing the fullbloods react the same way. They both clutched their seats and Andre, who was religious, signed the cross of the Maker.

They landed without incident but had to wait because it was still daylight. At dusk, after Sean had asked Andre and Dedreh to lay a netting over the runway to camouflage it, he came into the cabin and sat beside Lucien. He wore a black beret and a green uniform with a patch over the arm. The sigil was of a clenched fist. Sean was human, about forty years old with grey in his beard.

"Do not stay in Nocturne overnight. Do not visit their dens. Do not trust the Bloods or your own company," said Sean. "These are words Silverfox wanted me to relay to you."

These words, Lucien had already heard. The plane was parked in a hanger with the door raised and locked. "Do you know them?" Lucien asked about the two fullbloods accompanying him.

"They are Francis's men, Lucien, enough said." Sean clicked his tongue. "Do not trap yourself in Nocturne. Get the hell out of there before it's daylight, yeah?"

"Heard you," said Lucien.

"Is Madea all right or what, sending you here alone?" Sean tapped his temple. "They say she's not right in the mind."

"I know they say that." Lucien got up. His watch said nine in the evening. "If they come back without me, leave them here and report back to Silverfox, yeah?"

"Heard you," said Sean. They shook hands and Sean pulled Lucien's arm and bumped his forearm into his. "Vamperish immortalis." Sean saluted.

"All hail the Raven Queen." Lucien tapped his heart.

Resurgence and Ravens were allies in theory, and so were the Bloods—the three prongs of the Trinity—and resisted the faerie from taking over the rest of the world. Yet in reality, it was a petty game of factions. Lucien trusted Sean, but not the two fullbloods with him and they were supposedly all on the same side.

Lucien drove his black sedan out of the belly of Bluejay, the name of the passenger plane, and headed to Nocturne with Andre next to him and Dedreh in the back seat. He adjusted the rearview mirror so he could see Dedreh. Nine-thirty by the time they left the hangar, an hour drive to the catacombs, and the sun would rise at seven-thirty in the morning. Lucien had five hours, six if he wanted to push it, in Nocturne, before he had to be out of there. It was more than enough time to have a simple conversation, but having never been on a field mission the boiling pot in his chest spilled over and hissed. The pressure built and he exhaled as if he could vent out the steam of anxiety. Reaching over to the center console, he turned on the music to calm his nerves. He loved the twentieth century of human history, and Ella Fitzgerald's voice came on to soothe him.

"What's this shit anyway?" Dedreh asked, blowing out the red mist of *krystallis*.

"Jazz," Lucien answered.

"Music of the lost continent?" Andre asked.

The North and the South Americas were faerie territory. The first recorded occurrence of the faerie was at Groom Lake, a North American military base marked as 'Area 51'. Following the Bloodline War, much of the earth including the Asias was a nuclear wasteland.

"Music of the lost civilization," Lucien said.

"Voices of the dead creep me out. Shut it off," Dedreh said.

Lucien complied, and they were left with the sound of the windshield wipers swiping at low speed as an autumn rain began to fall. They were driving through the ruins of a great human city, one of the oldest, and Lucien took the roundabout, curving around a stone monument, a grand gate covered in vines.

"Arc de Triomphe," Dedreh murmured, his brown eyes rolling back into his skull from the diamorphine. "My father brought me here when I was a boy. There are names of the dead etched inside. From the human wars, I mean. It was before the Third War, and in those years we never thought there would be any other kind of war. Humans killed each other, that wasn't front-page news. But we were naive enough to believe that when the world ended, it would be of our doing."

"It *was* our doing," Andre said. "We opened the gateway to the faerie world." Whenever he said things like that, he signed the cross. "You ever hear of hell? Well, we opened the doorway to it. Demons were once angels, and that is what the faerie are, demons with white wings."

"Says your book?" Dedreh chuckled. "What say your Maker?"

"He says we deserve this."

"He's an asshole then," Lucien said, turning into the parking area in front of the entrance to Nocturne.

Dead faeries hung from poles like dried-out birds, had birds been six feet tall with eight-foot wings. The carcasses would have to be at least a century old, the last time the faerie crossed the Atlantic. Lucien circled and parked his car in a flooded lot, partially collapsed. There was rusted junk covered in moss all around him.

He covered his black sedan with shrubs and put the key in the glove compartment. It was the moment that he shut the door that he had foresight. A girl in a silver sequin dress with a tattoo of wings on her back stood in a dark hallway and held out a small pink pillow in her palm. When she turned, she had tattoos of swords on her arms. Bleached blonde hair, the dark roots showing, without saying a word she took his breath away. Lucien leaned on the hood of his car.

He could only foresee danger a split second into the future and only when it affected him. Queen Madea could see hours ahead but that was stupendous—she was extraordinary. Lucien was still outside and not in a dark hallway. A split second passed and he didn't see the girl. Perhaps his mind was tripping on secondhand diamorphine and methamphetamine from the red mist Dedreh had been exhaling throughout the entire flight, and then in the car.

"You all right?" Andre narrowed his eyes.

"It's fine." Lucien popped the collar of his black blazer. "Let's get it over with."

The five-mile descent to Nocturne was heavily guarded against the faerie and it comforted Lucien some. But on the other hand, there was no way of getting out of here should Vitali turn hostile. These things weighed on him as he made the walk down into the underground cesspool, the reek of stale urine slapping him in the face as he approached the last checkpoint.

A crimson-eyed Blood blinked at Lucien and his company from behind iron bars, demanding to see identification. Lucien held out his hand with the Raven ring. Polished silver, on purpose, with a black raven captured inside a red ruby—seal of the Raven queen.

"I'm Sedric." A man with a greasy ponytail and flowery silk shirt opened his arms for an embrace. "Welcome to Nocturne."

Lucien and his entourage expected to collect their weapons at the other side of the iron bars, but the gatekeeper remarked, "One edge is silver." He shot a look at Sedric. "You can't bring silver into Nocturne."

"The other edge is iron," said Lucien. "It's called the *reaper,* and it's the weapon we carry. We're not surrendering it. If you don't want to let us through, that is fine. But then you call Vitali here. I must insist on having a word with him on behalf of my queen."

"Give them their weapons," said Sedric. "We're all friends here."

Receiving his weapons belt, Lucien strapped it around his waist, the familiar weight of the *reaper* comforting him some. "Take us to Vitali."

"Of course," said Sedric. "Follow me."

The stale air, the stagnant water, and the reek of mold, mildew, and urine hung like an invisible fog in the dark corridors and coated the surfaces like a slimy film. The whole thing was repulsive to Lucien, but he tried not to be a child about it. A skin on skeleton, a man with a string of lights wrapped around his torso passed by Lucien on a skateboard and so pungent was his odor that he may as well be made of armpits that hadn't been washed in a century. His eyes watered from it.

Sedric wasn't much better for he smelled of days old sweat. Lucien tried not to touch anything and refused a seat when he was offered one in a cave looking room. The furniture was old, probably hauled in from the ruins above, and the cushions of the chairs were damp from Maker knew what. Vampires didn't shit, but they did piss when they drank something other than blood and there was a lot of it happening, as a woman with a pink skirt lifted it in the corner and squatted.

"Forsaken heathens," Andre mumbled and turned away.

"Are we done?" Dedreh shuddered. "You realize we breathe through the pores of our skin as well?"

Lucien flicked his wrist to check his watch: midnight. He had five more hours.

Sedric, who'd gone to fetch Vitali, returned with some Bloods who weren't Vitali, and settled down behind a rotted wooden table, spreading *krystallis* on a tray and crushing it. Then he ground it to fine dust with a playing card and portioned it into lines. Inevitably, he snorted a line, then grimaced and wiped his nose.

"Well?" Lucien tried to be patient. It was his first mission, and he didn't want to fail.

"Sad news, friends." Sedric smiled, still snorting and wiping his nose. "Do you know what pales are?"

"Yes," Andre answered.

Lucien shot him a look and the fullblood backed down, waving an apologetic gesture.

"Then you understand that they are extremely dangerous," said Sedric. He wore silver-toed boots and crossed his ankle over his knee. "There was a pale outbreak in Nocturne and Vitali went to address it. We apologize for the delay, but we must consider the safety of our people first. My brother will be back shortly, but in the meantime, enjoy our dens. On the house, of course."

"That's not ideal," said Lucien.

"That's life." Sedric shrugged. "Here, Raven, have a line. It's Nocturne's best." He offered the tray.

"I'd rather not."

"Never caught your name, what is it?" Sedric tipped his head to the side.

"Lucien."

"Lucien, you look young, so I'll forget the offense. But you're being rude. Or are you afraid that I'll bite you?" He grinned, flashing two yellowed fangs as long as tusks.

Without Silverfox around, Lucien didn't know what the proper etiquette was. He didn't want to offend the Bloods so early on, but he didn't want to be high in unfamiliar territory. In the end though, he walked to the table because Francis's men were weighing his worth, and the Bloods were witnessing.

"Vitali will come shortly?" he asked.

"As soon as possible." Sedric pushed the tray and held out a filthy straw.

Lucien drank clean blood and smoked clean blood. He was aware that this might hit him like a tidal wave when he smiled and took the straw from Sedric.

The trend of lacing narcotics with synthetic blood began with the Bloods but it wasn't a new concept with the Ravens either. It did seem to make hours vanish, however, and every time Lucien flicked his watch, another hour had passed without him accounting for it. Dedreh and even the frigid Andre seemed to be having a grand time at a den called the 'Heaven', drinking and smoking in the company of hostesses that crowded them. At four in the morning, three hours before dawn, when Vitali hadn't arrived, Lucien decided to call it a day and head out of Nocturne. His first mission would be a failure, something Francis would relish, but Silverfox had explicitly warned him not to stay overnight in Nocturne.

A woman other than Andre's wife was sucking on his earlobe, and Dedreh had disappeared with a hostess and hadn't returned. Lucien had been drinking whiskey, the one he brought from home, and he needed to piss. He left his two companions to make the best of it for the five minutes he needed to go find a latrine, and stepped out of Heaven alone. He got directions to the public latrine from the bouncer because he didn't want to relieve himself in a dark corner as some patrons had been. He was a Raven and not a fucken Blood. He didn't live in filth and wasn't accustomed to it either.

He'd been staggering as he passed by a stretch of a hallway with candles lit on the floor, and it felt familiar. So much so that it was a déjà vu—foresight. In this exact corridor, the patterns of candles on the floor like constellations he recognized, a bouncer with a scar over his left eye stood by a door to another den. Bald on the crown with a bear-shaped golden pendant dangling from his thick neck, he was exactly as Lucien had seen him, down to the red vest he wore under the black jacket. The girl wasn't there, and Lucien glanced into the den.

"Welcome to the Priest," the bouncer said.

"What?" Lucien blinked.

"You're the VIP? This den is called the Priest." The bouncer winked with his good eye. "You're welcome to it, on the house, of course." He all but bowed.

Lucien looked at the line of people trying to get in, but the girl he'd seen wasn't among them. Perhaps this was the wrong time, but what he'd seen had been a real foresight and not a dream. Hours out, it was not possible. He wanted to ask the bouncer about the girl in a silver sequin dress, but he didn't want to give out her identity. The ink on her back, the tattoos of wings, had been very prominent. Raven foresight was triggered *only* when the matter was significant, such as life-threatening.

He checked his watch—four-thirty in the morning. The sun would rise in three hours. An hour to get out of Nocturne, and an hour to drive back to the hangar. He should have left. This was the time to take his meager entourage, piss on his way out through the walk, and drive back to the hangar with barely enough time for Sean to be cursing him out.

Instead, Lucien said, "I have some friends with me. I'll go bring them."

The bouncer smiled and nodded.

Going against everything Silverfox had warned him about, Lucien headed back to Heaven, not to leave but to bring Andre and Dedreh to Priest. He *had* to know.

Queen Madea was his mother, but the Raven queen's mind was unraveling, and she hadn't been lucid for years. Lucien was twenty-four years old in a world of vampires hundreds if not thousands of years old. By Raven bylaws, one had to be at least a century old to rule, and his uncle, Queen Madea's younger brother Francis, had every reason to have Lucien silvered in a Blood den.

Silverfox was Lucien's father and he and Francis had been at each other's throats even before Lucien was born—they split the Raven court. Ravens didn't have parents, not as humans did, for they didn't rear their young, but the throne did follow a linear bloodline. Lucien was aware that he was a token in a war between Silverfox and Francis. Heeding his father's warning, he *should* leave Nocturne while he had time. Once the sun rose it wouldn't set for thirteen hours, and Lucien would be trapped underground—a long time should his host turn hostile.

Taking all this into consideration, he *still* had to know who the girl was and why he'd seen her so far out.

Priest

"Priest?" asked Eshe.

"Heaven," said Star.

"Playground," voted Kara.

Although there were countless pleasure dens in Nocturne, those three were run by Sedric personally and had the best clientele. Kara, Eshe, and Star drew straws and Kara's was the broken—Playground it was.

Kara had thick, black hair which Star had dyed platinum blonde in his effort to make her pretty, and in the jagged mirror Kara tucked her shoulder-length fried blonde hair behind her ears. She wore a white sequin dress with thin straps over the shoulder and two front slits that came up to her hips, showing naked skin where an undergarment line would be. Six-inch-heels, genuine leather, and she was still the shortest of the three.

Ready for the 'night', they sashayed through the maze of tunnels and crossed the Haze Hall where stoned vampires stared at images of the lost world projected on the tall wall. An image of a smiling man in a blue suit and tie sang and danced in silence. The ghosts had no sound.

Twenty miles of winding corridors, rooms with open doors on both sides, tattoo parlors, trinket vendors, candlemakers, tailors, shoeshiners, hairdressers, and endless others trying to earn their thousand *dinne* for a baggie of *krystallis,* and they arrived at Playground where a Blood bouncer checked Kara's fugly satchel for weapons at the door, then waved her in.

The catacombs had been constructed by the humans when they were building the great city above. They'd moved millions of remains from cemeteries and mass graves and had stuffed them underground, the city of bones, and at Playground the vampires had made a display of it. Human skulls and femur bones lined the walls like grey mushrooms, and small round tables were draped with ivory cloth. Candles were lit on the floor, and a large bed with an iron frame at the center furnished the den.

The den was half full, a crowd of about fifty vampires, and a dull techno beat thrummed through the wall of bones as Kara settled by the bar with the girls. They ordered a bottle of Nebula with the last of their *dinne* and the bartender set three glasses on the bar. To play, one must pay—den rules.

"Fancy a drink with me, honey?" Star wasted no time working on a thick male with a faux leather jacket.

Fullbloods stayed as they'd turned. The shoeshiner who also fixed the many heels Kara broke had been in his sixties and frail when he died, a thin man. The blonde bartender had been in her late teens, and the faux leather man in his forties, with thinning hair.

"What time is it?" Kara asked the faux leather man because he had a gold wristwatch, but he frowned, confused, and Star hissed. The faux man had forgotten what a watch was, and Star thought Kara was stepping on his toes—neither got the joke.

Never mind.

Eshe laughed at something one of the Bloods said, leaning in and gliding her hand up his thick thigh. Those who worked directly for the Blood brothers, Vitali and Sedric, were easy to spot with their matching black suits and gold chains and were called the 'Bloods'. Most inhabitants of Nocturne were mundane fullbloods like Star and Eshe who'd been turned by another fullblood. A silver dagger to the heart ended their immortality in a hurry, but true Bloods like the bouncer or the one Eshe was working on were nearly impossible to silver, with beastly strength and impenetrable skin. Only sunlight did them. Also, their pockets were heavy with *dinne*.

Not as pushy as Star and not beautiful like Eshe, Kara had been biding her time, sipping Nebula and staring at her lap, playing with the iron bangles she wore on both her wrists, when she heard, "Offer me a drink," and looked up.

A scrawny man with spiky hair smiled at her, his fangs yellow but his eyes bright like two holes in the layer of grey muck he was covered in—a scavenger. They crawled in and out of the twisting and turning tunnels of the catacombs, the size of a manhole at certain parts, and brought trinkets from the human ruins above.

"Sebastian." She returned the smile.

"Saw a thing and thought of you," said the scavenger, reaching into his mud-covered jacket, and pulled out a white mug with black letters and a red heart. 'I love Paris' it read, the heart standing for the love.

"It's beautiful," said Kara, reaching for it, but he slipped it back into his jacket.

"Offer me a drink," he said.

"I can't. I'm working. I don't want to get my clothes dirty."

"I have some *dinne.*" He looked around pretending to scan the crowd, hurt.

"How much?" she had to ask.

"Twenty."

That wasn't enough. Kara needed *krystallis* more than she wanted the heart. *'Stop trading yourself for tchotchke!'* Star would berate her, and he was right, but she still wanted the mug.

"I'll see you later. I just need to earn some. Keep the mug for me, yeah?"

"Nah," he said, turning. "I'd rather find *dinne* for it. I'm working too."

"Can I see it again?" Kara called after him, asking about the mug.

"No, girl, it's gone." And so was he.

Kara thought about running out after him, but Star's hand closed around her arm, the blue polished nails digging into her skin. He leaned in and whispered with a smile on his face, "Don't fuck with scavengers. I'd hate to lose a second roommate so soon."

She'd really wanted the mug, the red heart on it had been bright and unfaded. But oh well, Star was right.

When the last of the Nebula was gone, the bartender took the glasses, wiping her bar with a rag that smelled of recycled water. Eshe and Star had stepped out in the hallway several times each, disappearing into the dim with their companions, and returning with *dinne* to add to the pot. Kara had earned nothing, and she didn't expect the girls to share.

No drink, no play. The Nebula being gone, and Kara not having the *dinne* to purchase a glass, had to leave. She walked through the corridors of bones and dust, the light bulbs dangling overhead from black wires thinning, then disappearing altogether as she approached the fringes. The nocturnal eyes of the fullbloods passing her in the tight quarters glinted predator red. They were harmless, just scavengers, and she found Sebastian in one of the dark rooms with standing water on the floor.

Sebastian had a lantern hanging from a chain dangling from the ceiling—he was also halfblood. The light swayed a bit, making the shadows move.

"Do you have any *krystallis*?" Kara asked, settling down next to him on a dry rock.

"Yeah, if you earn it."

"Where do you get your hair cut?" she asked, stroking his spiky blond crown. "It's nice and even."

"Oh, I'm not spending *dinne* on that. I cut it myself." He got up to show her a clipper. It buzzed when he pressed the switch on it.

"Wow! You have batteries?" Kara wanted to see but he put it away.

"They have solar panels up there. I charge it in one of the ports." He stood in front of her. "So, you want some smoke or what?"

She did, and she let him fuck her standing up against the wall. There wasn't much in it for her, but he was nicer after he came and shared his diamorphine. He also let her have the cup with the heart.

"I'm going to Lyon during the eclipse," he said, handing her his pipe. "You can come with me if you want."

"That's nearly three hundred miles. You can't make it in three days," Kara said.

"You don't even know where it is," Sebastian said. "You've never even been up top, have you?"

"I wasn't born here."

"Whatever, you don't know. I have a bicycle."

"What's in Lyon?" asked Kara.

"Freedom."

It was the same venomous idea that had burned Celeste. But she said nothing. She didn't care about Sebastia like that. Matter of fact, she didn't care about anyone 'like that'. She didn't have a heart, not the metaphorical one or the physical one.

On her walk back to the Coeur, the lights eventually returning, Kara dug through her satchel to see if there was anything she could sell to be able to afford a drink at Priest—the den she was headed to. Nocturne was a cycle of earning *krystallis,* smoking it, then searching for more. They had a name for those who couldn't afford synthetic blood—pales. Well, she wouldn't turn pale. She could leave, but go where? Diamorphine was how she could stand being herself.

She decided on the one she could part with and stood in the limestone corridor, a few paces from the Priest's entrance, and solicited fullbloods going in and out, but no one wanted to buy her yarn heart.

"You can't do business like that," the bouncer came out and snarled. "You know better, Kara. Where's Star?"

"Home, probably." She shrugged.

"Go get him, then, and Eshe too. We're expecting some VIPs."

"What VIP?" Kara wanted in and tried to step around the bouncer but the Blood, whose name was either Darrel or Daren... or Derrick... or Eric, barred her way. He had one blind eye, was born that way, Kara supposed. Vampire injuries healed.

"Sorry, girl. You're too strung for this crowd." He scrutinized her up and down with the single eye. "Go find Star."

"If I do, can I get in?"

"No."

"Will you give me a fifty for it?" She held out the yarn heart on her palm. Maybe they wouldn't let her into Priest with the VIP and all, but fifty would buy her a drink at Heaven, the den she meant to visit next.

"No," said the bouncer.

"You made a pillow for a mouse?"

Kara turned to the voice and was face to face with a pureblood—the irises of his eyes were scarlet. He had soft brown curls and was dressed in frayed blue jeans and a white t-shirt, a black blazer over it, and his clothes were clean as if he didn't live in the tunnels. He cocked his head curiously. A dagger hung from his waist in a genuine leather scabbard.

The company he had, two males behind him, were also armed in the same manner but they were fullbloods with plain eyes.

"It's a heart," Kara said, holding her hand out so he could see.

"Well, that's sad," the pureblood said, then passed by Kara to enter Priest, his company following him. "Nice ink, by the way." He looked back, tapped his shoulder, then disappeared into the den.

Kara had a tattoo of wings on her back and two blades, one on each forearm, but he'd probably meant the wings since he'd tapped his shoulder.

"Come on, let me in!" Kara pleaded with the bouncer. Purebloods were rare, and Kara knew the three dozen who lived in Nocturne—he was not one of them. That was the VIP.

"No," hissed the bouncer. "Get lost!"

"Hey." The pureblood came out just as the bouncer was shoving Kara. "How much is the pillow?"

"It's a heart," insisted Kara. "Fifty."

"Here," he tossed her a coin. "Keep the change." Then disappeared again without taking the 'pillow'.

Kara didn't need to see to know the coin he tossed her was a hundred *dinne,* and she flashed it to the bouncer as she sashayed past him. She could pay, so she could play—den rules.

Nothing

The Priest had multiple rooms inside, layered like honeycomb, a combination of limestone walls and pillars the humans had erected an eon ago. The brick stairs the Bloods built connected the levels, and randomly found furniture from above populated the floors. The seats were mostly iron frames, plastic chairs, and stone slabs. Wood didn't age well down here. What made the space the 'Priest' was the crescent pool by the wall. Supposedly the water drained down from a cathedral above and was holy, and the drunk undead horsed around baptizing each other in it.

Some candles on the floor flickered and blinking strings of lights were wrapped around the pillars. Kara bought a glass of Nebula from the bar by the door and headed inside, looking to play. If a patron accepted a drink from a hostess, he was also willing to pay for pleasure. If he refused, the hostess must empty the drink herself, then go pay for another so she may solicit someone else. Not counting the Blood bouncers, there were about a hundred patrons in Priest, but Kara had two stabs at the thing before she was crap out of luck.

On her first try, she approached a shy man with a knitted vest, reading glasses on his face as if he read anymore. The undead clung to human habits, reading glasses, wristwatches, and other nuisances to feel less dead down in the catacombs. Kara wondered if it ever worked.

"Hello." She walked up to the reading glasses man sitting on the steps alone. "I'm Kara." She held out her hand, and he took it. His handshake was limp.

"I'm Steward." He smiled, adjusting his glasses—probably a nervous tick.

"Do you mind if I sit here?" she asked, sitting down already.

"Sure." He scooted to the side.

"Looking for company, honey?" Kara placed her hand on his knee and he blushed, staring down at his lap. "Do you want a drink, Steward?" She offered her cup.

"Oh, I'm with someone already. She went to get us more drinks." He gestured at the slew of hostesses by the bar. "I'm sorry."

A bouncer was watching, so Kara took her shot, tried to smile at the glasses man, then strutted to the bar to buy another try with her last fifty.

As she placed the coin on the bar and the bartender slid a glass of Nebula to her, Kara scanned the crowd for the pureblood but didn't see him.

"Did the VIP leave already?" she asked the bartender.

"No, they're at the back." He pointed with his chin as he wiped the bar. "I'm supposed to push the drinks and all, but you're not looking so well, Kara. Don't waste your offer on them. They're not looking to play. They turned down Eloise and if that girl is a ten, you're like a three. No offense, I'm just looking out for you."

"I know," said Kara.

He was being kind, but Kara took her drink and headed to the back anyway—this was why she was always broke and constantly teetering on the edge of sickness and withdrawal. Everyone was a ten except for her, and everyone knew it except for her.

At the corner of Priest, there was a small space like a collapsed cave called the Canary. It also led out to Teuf, a much larger room. But Teuf hadn't been used for some time because it was flooded with sliding muck. The mouth of the Canary was wide enough for only one to pass through and the pureblood's company guarded it. The blond was alone. Visibly high even in the dark, he gritted his teeth, clean fangs flashing as he grimaced. His hand rested on the hilt of his weapon when his attention shifted to Kara.

"Turn around and go back the way you came," he said.

"I have his heart." Kara showed the pink yarn heart.

"Piss off, woman."

"Oh, the mouse girl," came a voice from the Canary. "Let her through, Andre."

The serious blond stepped aside but confiscated Kara's satchel and gave her a thorough pat down as if she'd been wearing much. He inspected the bangles last, turning her hands to see that she wasn't palming anything. "Wrought iron?" He frowned about the bangles. "Why?"

"To keep the fae away." Kara smiled.

"Funny, this one," said Andre the serious blond, stepping aside to let Kara through.

The Canary glowed amber with so many candles lit it looked as if a swarm of fireflies had fallen on the ground. The pureblood was sitting on a stack of slabs that lined the wall like a long bench, and his other companion, a tall man with long red braids, was standing at the mouth that led out to Teuf, a black hole in the star-studded Canary.

"Here, you bought this." Kara handed the pureblood the yarn heart.

"What do you know? It is a heart," said the pureblood, showing the thing to the red braids who didn't look interested. He was about fifteen feet away. Maybe he couldn't see. "Do you want to sit?" asked the pureblood.

Kara, holding her glass of drink, needed no second invitation and sat down beside him. Lean built and barely taller than Kara when they passed in the hallway, the pureblood was small for a Blood male—the bouncers were twice his size. With soft features on his face, he'd be in his early twenties had he been human.

"Are you young?" Kara asked a thing that was none of her business. "You're the smallest pureblood I've ever seen," she blurted out. Had she been better at flirting, she wouldn't be always so 'strung out'.

The pureblood turned toward Kara, a smile twisting his lips, and both his companions laughed, the red braids grinning inside and the serious blond cackling outside the door.

"Met many purebloods, have you, girl?" asked the red braids, his voice as deep as the woofers of the den.

"Have a name, halfblood?" asked the pureblood.

"Good guess," she said about him calling her halfblood. "I'm Kara."

"Not a guess, I can smell the human on you a mile away. Not that unpleasant, I must admit." He held out his hand. The sleeve of his blazer was pristine black with hardly any dust on it, and his nails were clean. "I'm Lucien." He had a strong and warm grip.

"Nice to meet you, Lucien. Do you want a drink?" She offered the glass.

"You mean the shit brew here? No, thank you."

Damn, but she didn't know if he understood the den rules. Kara should take her shot now and call it a day but there were no bouncers around to throw her out, so she held onto her drink... till Lucien took the glass from her and tossed the Nebula on the floor. A candle fizzled from the spray. More recycled water than ethanol, Nebula wasn't flammable.

"Dedreh, give her a real drink," said Lucien.

The red braids reached into the hemp satchel slung across his body and produced a flask. Steel inside but the brown leather sleeve was beautiful.

"Where do you come from?" Kara asked. The things they had were clean and new, not upcycled, downcycled, repurposed, or recycled for a century.

"Doesn't concern you," said Dedreh, pouring a burnt amber colored liquid into the glass that Lucien had emptied.

"Thank you," Kara said, taking it.

A whiff told her it was liquor, but the sip was strange, tasting of wood, herbs, and smoke from fire. "What is this?" she asked.

"Whiskey," said Lucien.

"It tastes like outside. Do you come from outside?" she asked.

"I believe Dedreh already answered you." Lucien pulled out a glass vial from his blazer pocket, red crystals inside, and Kara shivered with the need. "Did you want to smoke?" he asked.

"Can I?"

"Sure. Here." He handed her his pipe as well, thick, hand-blown glass with a raven painted on the stem—everything he had was pretty.

Not wanting to appear like a blood-fiend Kara tried to be casual, but as she loaded and lit the *krystallis*, holding a candle flame underneath the glass bowl, she inhaled deeply and expected the high to hit as she exhaled the red mist.

But nothing happened.

She inspected the *krystallis*. "Is this weak?" she asked, loading another hit.

"It's clean," said Lucien. He was watching her.

"What?"

"Nothing." He bit his lower lip and she didn't know what for. She didn't know him and couldn't read him. "Dedreh, step out for a moment."

The braids took his time adjusting his belt and making disapproving faces, and when he finally crossed the Canary and stepped out to the Priest, he muttered, "Try not to bond with a whore."

Lucien snapped, growling after Dedreh, his scarlet eyes burning with fury.

"Are you all right?" Kara asked, tasting a bit more of the whiskey. It was an acquired taste, and she was acquiring it quickly.

"I'm sorry. I didn't mean to frighten you." The chestnut brown locks with soft waves had fallen over his face.

"You didn't," Kara said, reaching over to tuck a stray strand of hair behind his ear. Vampires didn't scare her, and besides, fear was for those with hearts to race as wildly as his was when she glided her fingers down the side of his neck.

She opened her hand and pressed it on his chest. Through the thin cotton of his shirt, she felt his heart pound against her palm. Holding each other's gaze, they were breathing in tandem as Lucien closed his eyes. A moment passed, then with a sharp inhale, he opened his eyes and removed Kara's hand, setting it on her lap as if it was a thing he was returning.

"What time is it?" she asked, seeing that he wore a wristwatch with a leather band.

He flicked his wrist, then cursed. "Seven in the morning."

Kara grabbed his hand and looked at his watch. The long hand was moving. "Where did you get this?" she exclaimed. She brought it to her ear, and it ticked. "Wow!"

He laughed, cupping her cheek, another unintentional thing he did, till he realized what he was doing and pulled his hand away, stuffing it into his pants pocket. "If you like it, you can have it when I leave."

"When are you leaving?"

"Not for another thirteen hours." More mumbled curses followed.

"You don't like it here?" she asked.

"It's not that... where is Vitali, do you know?"

Kara shook her head. "Lucien?"

"Yeah?"

"Can you buy me *krystallis?* Do you have any *dinne?*"

"Sure." He rose, dusting off his pants. "Do you want to show me around? Since I'm stuck here anyway, may as well see what it's all about."

"Of course." Kara finished the whiskey, set the glass down, and got up as well. The first place she wanted to show him was the blood kiosk down the hall. She charged two hundred and fifty to host.

The Bloods didn't allow the hostesses to solicit patrons outside of the dens—they wanted their cut, and leaving with a patron cost a hundred *dinne* at the door and the bouncer demanded three hundred because of the two fullbloods with them. Lucien handed the coins to Kara and when she went to pay the bouncer, he told her to take it to the bar.

"I'll be right back." Kara waved at Lucien who was speaking with Andre.

He nodded.

When Kara stepped back into Priest, the bouncer followed her in and yanked her arm, shoving her against the wall. He was large and she felt his weight as he leaned against her to whisper, "The pureblood."

He shoved a little bag into her hand when he took the coins. Kara looked down at it. A plastic baggie of round white tablets—den roofie. "I don't do that," she said.

She tried to stuff the baggie into the bouncer's jacket pocket, but he twisted her wrist. "Vitali ain't asking. Feed it to the pureblood and win fifty thousand *dinne,* that's a fuck load of *krystallis* for you blood-fiends. But yap about it, you'll win a walk in the sun."

He shoved her out the door, and when Kara stumbled out, her heel catching a crack on the floor, Lucien turned to her. "Everything all right?"

"All set." Kara palmed the baggie, dropping it into her fugly satchel. She beamed her best smile because at least her teeth were clean. Even the Maker's children betrayed each other. So, what were three strangers to her who had no heart to weep for Celeste?

Nothing. They meant nothing.

Kara gouged Lucien, making him buy her a thousand *dinne* baggie. The Blood behind the iron bars had a tattoo of a snarling bear on his bald head, and he tossed the baggie on a scale to show Kara it was indeed 3.5 grams before pushing it through the bars.

He gestured for the next, and as Kara and Lucien moved out of the way Eloise stepped up—she was a ten. "You know..." She eyed Lucien, tossing her hair. "The going rate in a den is two hundred and fifty."

"My shoes cost fifteen thousand," said Lucien. "I'm sure you're worth more."

Eloise said nothing but blushed. The Blood yelled for the next and she moved up the line, counting the change of *dinne* on her palm. She didn't have enough, and Kara saw it. She fished out the largest shard from her bag and put it on Eloise's palm, who batted her eyes, looked confused, then mumbled, "Thank you."

Kara glanced at Lucien's shoes as they headed away from the kiosk queue. Genuine leather white sneakers with beautiful stitching and flowers painted on the side, they weren't upcycled. Someone had made

them for him especially. She would believe they were fifteen thousand *dinne.*

As she showed Lucien around Nocturne, the two fullbloods a few
paces behind weren't the only ones following. Vitali's men were all
around, posed as things they were not, and keeping an eye on them.
She first noticed it in a tattoo parlor with buzzing neon lights on
the wall. She and Lucien were flipping through the artist's portfolio
book when she saw Jai, Vitali's goon, posing as a patron. Once she
noticed, she saw them everywhere. Andre and Dedreh couldn't tell
because they wouldn't know the pureblood in a trinket shop looking
at a model car was Josephine who hated humans and junk in equal
parts. She would never buy a model car or be in a trinket shop—she
was also Vitali's mate. She silvered hostesses out of jealousy when
Vitali showed interest in them beyond the single encounter that was
often the audition for the position.

"The catacombs are about two hundred miles in total," said Kara,
her high heels knocking on the limestone flooring with each step.
"But it's collapsed in many parts, then dug around. In some places,
you can barely crawl through. If you're not careful you can get stuck,
get lost, and go mad. The entryways shift over time, new holes appear
in the eroded walls, and doorways that used to exist disappear. It's
a great spiderweb with many dead ends and cut-off parts no longer
accessible from where we are.

"The dens, the rooms, the stores, and the kiosks, we call that Le
Coeur. It is the heartbeat of Nocturne. But out in the fringes, in the
dead veins, pales sometimes nest. Sometimes it's people who used to
live here but lost their minds, and other times its pales from above
seeking shelter from the sun. Either way, they're feral. They hunt
and eat each other and drink the blood of rats and wild animals who
wander down here.

"My friend Sebastian says the pales are afraid of light and sounds. He's a scavenger and they carry a boombox when they travel through the dark ends of the catacombs. Playing music keeps the pales away…"

"Boombox?" Lucien asked, gesturing a large thing carried on the shoulder.

"No." Kara illustrated the size of the tiny speaker.

The way she led them had flooded, not completely impassable but the hallway had standing water, grey muck about knee high. She looked at Lucien's white sneakers, and Andre and Dedreh's genuine leather boots.

"It does that sometimes," she said about the flood, turning around. "We'll go another way."

Lucien had asked her about the pales. He wanted to get as close to a nest as possible. Some parts of Nocturne had electric circuit breakers and others did not. It depended on the flood situation as well, and most of the catacombs turned dark when it was rainy season above.

"This way," she said instead, turning into the Hall of Arcs. Five different tunnels intersected here, and she led them down the one with white stripes painted on the columns—a warning for pales up ahead.

"If we run into them," she continued, "they are deadly. Why do you want to see them, anyway?" Kara threw a look over her shoulder to see Lucien. He was staring into a dark archway.

"What is that way?" he asked.

A red bear was spray painted on the wall beyond the arch he was looking at.

"Blood den," Kara said. "You're not allowed that way unless you're Blood. That's where they brew *krystallis*. They'll silver you on sight if you trespass."

"Are you sure?" Lucien asked. "Is it possible the pales breached the brewery?"

"It is the most guarded place in Nocturne," Kara said. "I highly doubt it."

"What is it, Lucien?" Andre asked, looking in the direction Lucien was.

"Nothing," Lucien said after a long while. "I must be wrong."

"Try not to be," Andre said, and they hissed at each other.

Back at Priest, Kara took off her heels and rubbed her feet while she waited at the bar. She'd walked around for a long time.

"Here you are." The bartender placed a bottle of Nebula and glasses on the tray. "On the house, of course."

Kara slipped back into her heels, carried the tray, and headed back to Canary. The fullbloods were no longer guarding the entrance and were chatting with hostesses instead, bragging about their weapons, and accepting drinks. The one called Dedreh smoked a lot and shared his *krystallis,* making him an instant attraction.

Lucien was alone in Canary. The candles had been refreshed since they were here last, and it was brighter. Kara weaved around the little flames on the floor and moved a candelabra from a stack of bricks to set the tray down. Her back to Lucien, she dropped one tablet into the glass and poured Nebula over it. For a beat, the tablet fizzled, then disappeared completely.

"A drink?" She turned.

"No, thank you." Looking down, he was flicking dust from the hem of his blazer mindlessly.

"Lucien?"

"Yeah?" He looked up, blinking.

"Please have a drink with me."

He took the drink and set it down.

"Do you know what the den rules are?" She sat down next to him, close enough for their legs to be touching. "When a hostess offers you a drink, it's an invitation to play."

"I can't. I'm sorry."

"Why?"

"You're stunning."

Kara laughed. He was funny. But because he looked confused, she asked, "You serious?"

He was.

"Why?" Now, she was confused.

"Are you asking me why you're beautiful?"

Then, she realized she didn't know what she was asking. The techno beat in Priest picked up tempo, and the crowd hooted. A drunk woman stumbled into Canary, said, "Oh, sorry," then staggered out.

"Look," said Lucien but he didn't point or say anything for another long while. A whole song passed by where the DJ did little else than scratch. Kara knew the DJ. He'd beat Star once for not giving him an 'in-house' discount. All the hostesses avoided him, and many complained to Sedric. But Jay was the only man willing to play the same techno beat for eternity.

"I've never met a halfblood before," he said. "Are there many more like you here?"

They were rare but not unheard of, vampire ones anyway.

"My friend Sebastian is halfblood. Would you like to meet him?"

"No."

The silence was so long that Kara fidgeted. "Do you mind if I smoke?"

"No, go ahead."

That was good. She occupied herself with loading her pipe and breathing the red mist till she thought she was flying. She missed flying. Soaking up sunlight above cotton white clouds, floating in the blue heaven where the Maker lived.

"I miss the sun," she whispered before she realized she'd said it out loud.

Lucien hadn't heard her. He was kicking dirt onto a candle that was burning out with an odd fume.

"It's this place, isn't it?" Kara asked. "You're not used to being intimate in public. I can find us a private place if you'd like." She pointed at the dark mouth of Teuf.

He glanced at where she'd pointed to then looked down, concerned with the candle again. "It's not that. Look," he said again but this time, elaborated, "I don't want you to think I'm an asshole. I haven't lived long, so it may not be worth much, but you're the most beautiful thing I've ever seen in my life. Pureblood Ravens mate for life and we risk bonding when we're intimate with someone we... like.

"But you're not a Raven. Even if, hypothetically, you liked me, you can't reciprocate my bond. Then I'll be a fool, pining forever for someone who doesn't want me. I can't risk that. Not even with another Raven because that's a game of power we play with each other. It involves a lot of trust, and I don't have it, not for anyone."

"You're a Raven?" Kara didn't care about the bond or the drink or Vitali. All she heard was *Raven*. "You're a Raven? Show me."

"What do you mean?" he asked.

"You should have ink on your arm, a Raven mark. I want to see it." She tapped her forearm.

Lucien got up and slipped out of the blazer. The white T-shirt he wore underneath was short-sleeved, and when he turned his arm, there were three black birds in flight on the inside of his forearm. Kara yanked his arm to see it closer, then looked up at him.

"You're a Raven," she breathed.

"Yeah, we're a covenant of the Trinity. The other is Resurgence," he said. "Did you think there was only Bloods?"

She'd known Ravens and the Resurgence existed during the Bloodline War but she hadn't heard of them since and thought perhaps they'd died, gone pale like the nest in Lyon.

"I want to be human," she said, forgetting herself, forgetting who she was talking to and where she was. "Can you help me?"

He ran his hand along the curves of her face, then whispered, "You're crying."

"I want to be human. Can you do that?" She didn't care about her broken eyes and blinked away the blur. The wet ran down her face.

"I can't *make* you human," he said, pulling his arm from Kara and putting his blazer back on. "I can make you *believe* you're human. But I won't do that."

"Why?" she pleaded.

"Humans walk in daylight and eat food. The minute you try to do either of those, you'll die." Lucien sat down, staring at one of the candles.

Kara could do both of those. Green apple was her favorite and she recalled the sourness of the bite on the inside of her cheeks. Her mouth salivated, making her realize it had been dry. But she couldn't tell him she was a faerie halfblood. That required *a lot* of trust and, just like him, she didn't have it, not for anyone.

"Tell me more about it," she said instead. "I've never met a Raven before but I heard of you. You can alter the mind, can you not?"

"Our talents are different from one another," said Lucien. "And the effectiveness varies, of course. What you're asking is called *weaving*. It's erasing old memories and creating new ones in their place. And I *can* do that, yes, but I don't like to."

"Why?"

"Once, I *weaved* a young girl's memory because a man had hurt her. It wasn't to help her but to protect the man. He was a Raven elder, one of my uncle's men. So, I *weaved* her mind, and she doesn't remember the hurt, but it stays here." He tapped his temple. "And now I carry it around. I *weave* only if my queen compels me, and most of the time, it's mundane shit, like information. But I hate it, still. It's like implanting another's voice into my being."

"What happened to the man?" Kara asked.

"I tried to silver him. I failed. And the queen ordered me to pull out my fangs with pliers. That was my punishment."

"You have your fangs."

"I was thirteen at the time. They only took a couple of weeks to grow back."

"So, the man still lives?" Kara asked.

"No, my father silvered him because he did it again to the same girl. And that's also the problem with forgetting hurt, Kara. You'll no longer remember who hurt you. You'll smile at him when he comes to your house and follow him out into his car."

"Why do you think I'm hurt?" Kara felt her brows knotting.

He was going to say something unkind. She saw him swallow back the words that had climbed up his throat. Instead, he said nothing and found interest in the candelabra. The orange flame reflected in his scarlet eyes and the mixture was—stunning.

He hadn't called her a 'whore'. Not in that exact term, but that was what dropped on his tongue. He was going to reference where she worked to why he thought she was hurt. But he wouldn't say that because he was kind. He had a heart that worked and that was why the candlelight made him beautiful. Kara didn't see so well in the dark, but she could see fine just then.

"Lucien, I have to go." She got up. She took the Nebula he'd set down and tossed it out. "It's really made from recycled piss. Don't drink the local brew."

"Have I offended you?" he asked.

"No, I just have to go."

"I can't make you think you're human because that will kill you. But whatever your hurt is, I can carry it, so you don't have to," he said. "If I promise you that, will you stay?"

Kara looked at the exit but her feet remained tied to the dirt in Canary. He couldn't promise her that, because as soon as he saw in her mind that she was a faerie, he wouldn't help her. He would kill her. She'd always hoped that if she ever met a Raven that he could fix her, but she hadn't known that he'd need to see into her mind first. She'd thought it might be a spell, but that was silly, of course. Vampires didn't have magic, only faerie. Yet she'd hoped anyway, but that was gone now.

"You're crying," he said again. "I didn't mean to offend you. Please stay." He got up and came closer.

Kara was five-four, so he was probably five-eight, not much taller. She was at eye level with him in her heels. He took her hand and she let him... before she yanked it.

"I have to go, and so should you."

"It's daylight outside," he whispered. "And I need to see Vitali."

"Bye, Lucien."

She walked out. She had to. She didn't want to be part of whatever was in Vitali's plan.

Stay

Kara saw Star sitting on the limestone ledge of the holy pool, Eshe play-fully dunking a patron's head into the red water behind him. Star looked tired and was rubbing his feet, the high heel dangling from his fingertip. On her way to Star, Kara tripped on a brick and kicked a candle that had been on the floor. It rolled and nearly burned a man wearing sandals. He hissed and Kara apologized. Vampires hated fire but they couldn't see in the pitch dark either. Most of the power breakers were out because of the flood and Nocturne didn't have electricity. The candlemakers made pretty *dinne* when it rained above.

"I'm going to go home," Kara said to Star.

"So, did you get paid or what?" he asked. "Everyone here is saying you're hosting the VIP."

"Here." Kara took out the baggie from her fugly satchel and emptied half the *krystallis* on Star's palm. "I'll see you at home."

"Bitch," Star started excitedly, but his expression changed to fear at something he saw over Kara's shoulder. He quickly fixed his long, blue hair, cleared his throat, and ran off, grabbing Eshe with him.

"Star?"

Kara turned right into Vitali's gold chain with a bear pendant. He was nearly a foot taller than her. Keeping her gaze down, she tried to step around him, but he barred her way. She took a deep breath and tilted her head back to meet his glowering crimson gaze.

"You have friends." He had a deep voice and smelled of the leather jacket he was wearing. The spikes on his jacket were iron. Like Sedric, he had a ponytail and bushy, dark brows. "Would you like me to walk them in the sun, these friends of yours?"

Kara shook her head.

"Then why be difficult? Have I not been kind, taking in a stray like you?"

She nodded, then looked down to stare at the skull on his belt buckle, but that was too close to the bulge under it, so she bowed her head further and settled on his silver-tipped crocodile skin boots.

"Was it so long ago that you showed up at my doors, shaking like a little lamb scared of the wolves? Halfblood and no gift, the boys would have made meat out of you had I not granted you my protection. Do you remember?"

She recalled fucking him for the said protection, and Sedric too, as all girls who worked in their dens did, but she didn't mention it and nodded. They were rough because vampires, even halfbloods, were durable and that was Nocturne. It was Blood territory and everyone in the catacombs belonged to Vitali. He'd once chained up a woman till she turned pale because she refused him. No one refused Vitali.

"Then why do you test my kindness, halfblood?"

"I tried," she said with a small voice. "He doesn't trust me and won't drink anything I give him."

He tipped her chin up with a finger, cocking his head when their eyes met. "You don't want to fail me, halfblood."

Kara shook her head. She wasn't afraid of him, but it was better to act subservient around him. Nocturne was her home, and she didn't want to jeopardize it.

"Order a drink," he said, and even before Kara asked, the bartender complied, setting a glass of Nebula on the counter and bowing to Vitali. "You have a thing in your bag. Take it out and drop it in the drink."

Kara glanced in the direction of Canary, but it wasn't visible from where they were. Dipping her hand in her satchel, she found the bag of roofies. She dropped the white, round tablet into the drink.

"More," Vitali said, and she dropped a second tablet. "More."

She dropped the third and Vitali nodded. He put his large finger into the glass and stirred the drink. Nebula was clear but now Kara's glass was murky. She hoped Lucien knew what the drink was supposed to look like, but it was unlikely because he wasn't from Nocturne. Where did he come from? Kara had never known where the Ravens lived.

"Come on, then." He draped his heavy arm around Kara's shoulders, and they crossed the floor together, everyone moving out of their way as four Bloods as large as Vitali followed.

Andre had appeared by the door again. He'd been looking back over his shoulder into Canary, but turned straight and dropped his hand to his hilt when he saw the Bloods approach. "You'd better be Vitali."

"So I am." Vitali opened his arms as if they were friends. Then he shoved Kara forward because the mouth of the Canary was too large for a group to enter at once.

In the cave of candles as if the stars had fallen on the floor Lucien, straddling a pile of limestone, had been speaking with Dedreh standing by the entry to the Teuf. Both turned as Kara entered, Vitali and his goons after her.

"Vitali," the Blood said, extending his hand to Lucien, who didn't get up to greet him. But the purebloods shook hands.

"Lucien."

"Sorry to keep you waiting. Had to deal with pales all day," said Vitali, settling down on a pile of rocks across Lucien.

Lucien shot a look at Kara and the drink she was holding but said nothing.

"It's a bit crowded," said Andre who'd followed them in. "Can some of your boys step out? We're all friends here."

"Sure." Vitali motioned for the Bloods to step out.

Andre exited with the Bloods, and it was Dedreh, Lucien, Vitali, and Kara in Canary. She found herself a seat by the door and set the glass down next to her. She hoped that she'd become invisible for none of this was her business.

"How is Madea?" Vitali asked.

"Well," was Lucien's answer.

"That's not what I hear." Vitali cackled, then reached over to the slab of stone with a drink tray on it and poured himself a glass.

"You heard wrong," said Lucien, casually loading a pipe as Dedreh observed them with his back pressed against the wall.

"Right, right." Vitali downed a glass of Nebula like a shot. "The queen is well and I'm a virgin. So, why do you come here? What do you need from me?"

Lucien parked his gaze on Kara. "Should she be here?"

"She's one of my best girls," Vitali said. He wouldn't say her name because he didn't remember it. "And I have a feeling whatever you're about to ask is not going to remain a secret for long."

"Right." Lucien lit his pipe, exhaling red mist. "The queen calls for war. Will the Bloods answer?"

Vitali tutted, displeased. "Francis is bloodthirsty. Why stir trouble when none exists?"

"It's not Francis. It's your queen who calls you."

"Right, and I was born yesterday." Vitali grimaced, pouring himself another glass. "It's about the Longdark, isn't it? Francis wants to assault Groom Lake during it? How is this time going to be different than the last? You seem young. Do you know many died in the Bloodline War?"

"Considering it was a world-ending event, billions," said Lucien.

"Right. Now, tell me how this is different."

"I'm not at liberty to say unless you're swearing your allegiance to the queen as your father did."

"Let's pretend it's Madea in charge, Lucien, and not Francis, an aristocrat who can't flick the piss from his dick," said Vitali. "In the best case scenario, Madea is asking me to trust her blindly when she got my father silvered. Is that right?"

"I thought Whiteswoon ambushed your father," said Lucien. "So, will you answer your queen's call?"

"Blood word is Blood life. I must think on it, Lucien. Let me discuss it with my clan. It's not a thing I can decide on my own. It's their lives too," said Vitali, to which Lucien nodded.

"How long will that take?" Lucien asked.

"Not long. When I call, they come. I'll give my answer shortly." Vitali motioned for Kara to get up, and she did. "In the meanwhile, my girl offers you a drink. Don't hurt her feelings."

"I don't want to drink your local shit, Vitali. Everything in your city smells of stale piss, no offense."

"Do you know what the den rules are?" Vitali grinned.

"I do and I've already said no." Lucien was indifferent and cold as Kara stood there holding her drink.

"Do you want a different, more refined girl? Or a boy?" asked Vitali. "My people told me you've taken a liking to this one but if they were wrong, I have better girls."

"Kara, sit down," said Lucien.

"No," said Vitali. "If she's not needed here she'll leave and go earn her *dinne*. I have other patrons who need servicing."

Kara remained standing where she was. This would be humiliating had she had any feelings. But she didn't. So who cared?

"She can stay, I don't mind her company. But stop offering me a fucken drink because I'm not doing that."

"What you do with her time is your business, Lucien. But if you want the girl's company, you have to accept a drink from her. Den rules." Vitali shrugged.

"You're really pushy with your shit brew," said Lucien, eyeing Vitali.

"It's not that bad." Dedreh had been drinking.

Lucien hesitated. He had a knack for sensing when things weren't right, but he was too young and didn't trust himself. He looked about twenty and Kara didn't think his blood age was much older.

"Fine," said Vitali. "The girl owes me *dinne*. It's best that she go earn it." He turned Kara to the door and slapped her ass. "Out you go."

She had no qualms about leaving and was almost out the door when she heard Lucien call her. "Kara, how much do you owe him?"

Nothing. Kara owed Vitali nothing but had to stall by the door because a Blood bouncer had appeared on the other side, wagging his fat finger at her.

"Five thousand," lied Vitali.

Kara may not have sympathy, kindness, or love but she did have rage and it burned her chest and throat as if she'd vomited pure ethanol. She wanted to pull Vitali's heart out through his mouth and chew it raw. The bouncer outside the door, she considered twisting his head clean off his body. She wanted to find Josephine and rip her guts out, and bash Sedric's skull in with the silver bat that Bloods carried.

Kara patted her wrist to see that the iron cuffs were still there, and they were. From time to time, she thought of harm which she hated because it reminded her of her father. She didn't want to be like him.

This is my home. I don't want any trouble. Kara took a deep breath and turned, managing a smile.

"Here." Lucien placed a stack of *dinne* in between himself and Vitali. "She's paid her debt. Now go have your town meeting. We are leaving in an hour." He checked his watch. "If you're not back by then, I'll take your answer to be no."

"Sure." Vitali turned to the door. "Enjoy yourselves. I'll be in before then."

"Good," said Lucien, then added, "You forgot your coins."

Like a servant, Vitali stooped, collecting the *dinne*. He was seething, and Kara could feel it.

"That's for me, I suppose?" Lucien asked just as Vitali was leaving, and the Blood threw a look over the shoulder to see Lucien take the glass from Kara's hand and down it.

A wicked satisfaction danced on the Blood's face before he stepped out.

"Why did you do that?" Kara whispered, frowning at the empty glass in her hand, the residue of the roofie like a calcium deposit on the rim.

Lucien took the glass from Kara's hand and set it on the drink tray. He pulled her by the back of the neck. His hand was warm but not hot, pleasant like evening sunlight. "Because I wanted you to stay."

Hate

The fullbloods vanished as soon as Vitali left. They were too fucked and past caring about security beyond pretense. That was why Vitali had tied them here for all this time. It was so the fullbloods would be buying the bar and drinking it too while Lucien was alone, trying to set a glass down and fumbling it.

"Fuck," he whispered, rubbing his face. "That shit is kind of strong, yeah?" He stretched out his legs, moaning a little as he closed his eyes. "Come sit with me. Please?"

Kara did.

But she had a lot on her mind. She didn't want to be a witness to Vitali silvering another pureblood. Then again, the whole of Nocturne had seen Lucien. If he was willing to silver a Raven messenger, it meant they weren't a threat to him. Vitali wasn't a fool.

So, when Lucien said, "You should come with me, Kara. This is no way to live," it meant nothing to her.

"Go where?" she asked, loading her pipe. She'd decided on bailing as soon as Lucien fell asleep.

"Home," he whispered with a deep sigh.

"I live here. This is my home."

"Did you know?" he asked, slurring his words. "I saw you hours out, and that's never happened to me before."

"Sure."

He laid down in her lap, and she stroked his soft crown. When his scarlet eyes opened, they were hazed over. "There is a lot going on right now. But when that is over, I'd like to see you again." His lids were too heavy, and he succumbed to the weight. "Can I see you again?"

"Sure." Kara traced her index from his jawline, over his lips, up over his nose to his forehead. "My father is Whiteswoon." She said the faerie king's name knowing that he was too far gone to remember it. He hardly reacted to her touch. "He kidnapped my mother, glamoured her, then forced her to have me. It's true that the faerie magic wanes during the eclipse and if you're mounting an offensive during the Longdark, I hope you kill him.

"The last eclipse, you probably don't know because you're too young, was sixteen years after the end of the Bloodline War. When the moon's shadow fell on the sun, and the midday turned to dusk, Whiteswoon's glamour failed and my mother woke up.

"She tried to kill him. We didn't have any wrought iron at home, you see, so she trapped him in the basement and set the mansion on fire. But he didn't die, wasn't even hurt. He caught her and just ripped her skin off as if it had been a cloak she'd been wearing.

"I remember that. I remember how her heart still beat in her naked ribcage. He let her lie there like a butchered animal, then he pried her ribs open, pulled out her heart, and ate it. I remember the wet chewing sound and the blood on his hands. I hate him, you see? I hate my father. I hate the faerie. I hate myself because I'm like them. I want to be human like my mother. I want to have a heart and be beautiful. But I'm just fugly and that's all.

"Whiteswoon is incredibly hard to kill. I'm sure you know that, your queen has been trying for... since the war. He has enchanted armor that you can't dent. It's highly unlikely you'd catch him without it on, but here's a secret." Kara bent down and kissed Lucien's forehead. Breathing deeply, he was out. "Faerie wings don't grow back if you tear them off. And even when he's armored, his wings must be out. Because as you know, the faeries fly.

"Goodbye, Lucien."

Kara got up, gently placing his head on the stack of limestone he was sleeping on—and left, this time for good.

She kept her head down as she passed a dozen Bloods in the hallway, Vitali leading them and a silver bat dangling from his grip.

Star and Eshe were building their house of cards when Kara went back to the place where she kept her things. She emptied her pouch over their cards and the coins rained down, all fifty thousand. A thousand *dinne* was large, round and some rolled on the dirt like wheels, disappearing into the dark corners.

"Are you fucken insane!" Star screamed, crawling on hands and knees to chase the coins.

Eshe scrambled on the dirt as well, her beautiful knees scabbing on the broken glasses and centuries-old debris that they lived on. Some were jagged bits of human bones that had been kicked around Nocturne for an eon.

While the girls hoarded their newfound wealth, paranoia sweeping over them as they worried about being silvered and robbed, Kara collapsed on Celeste's bed and folded into herself. She pulled up her knees to her chest because she was shivering from the pain in her chest. She didn't know what it was but it hurt.

It hurt, and hurt, and hurt, and wouldn't dull no matter how much she smoked. By the time she was screaming into some dirt, she was alone. Star and Eshe had buried most of the *dinne* and left to spend a bit of it. Everyone needed an upcycled dress once in a while.

Kara was sick. She'd fallen ill. It felt as if she'd pried her own chest open and stuck her wrought iron bangles into it. The hurt dulled a bit when she got up and felt even better when she began packing all her tchotchke hearts into her fugly satchel. She knew she wasn't coming back, and there, the pain went away.

"Thank you for taking me in, and thank you for being my friends," Kara said to the empty corner where her roommates erected their dream house out of cards.

She shoved the fifty *dinne* into the bouncer's hand and stormed into Priest. Vitali hadn't made a show of it, she guessed, because the den was the same with the same music, the same bartender, the same hostesses, and the same patrons. No one minded her as she crossed the floor and headed to the Canary. Andre was gone and two Bloods manned the entry instead. That meant Vitali was still there, and that meant Lucien probably was as well. Good enough.

Kara marched out of Priest and sprinted through the catacombs once she was out of sight of the Bloods. Although the entrances and exits were always shifting, she knew her way around reasonably well and was going to come through the Teuf side of Canary. It meant a lot of crawling on hands and knees, treading through puddles in the dark. It was good that she had a flashlight with batteries that she'd gotten from Sebastian. His other half was a vampire, and he could see in the dark almost as well as them, so he hadn't needed it.

Kara crawled through a collapsed tunnel and dropped down, landing in ankle-deep water in the dark. Only then, it occurred to her that she should have changed out of her silver sequin dress. But high as fuck, she was barely functioning, and clothes hadn't been on her mind.

The mouth of Canary, a slit of light, glowed like an open eye in the darkness of Teuf. She saw Vitali seated on a pile of rocks and smiling, a drink raised to his lips. Tripping on a thing, Kara shone the flashlight while shielding the brightness with her hand. It was Andre lying in shallow water. He was missing his head, but Kara knew the body was his because Dedreh was next to him, the red braids a bright vein in the black muck. Smashed to bits, crumpled like paper, he was gone.

Most of faerie magic was instinct ingrained in the blood that circulated despite having no heart. But she was trained as well, by Whiteswoon himself. In hindsight, he'd only done it to spite her mother but it was on him that he'd raised an enemy with inherited abilities.

Vitali saw her first and rose, grabbing his bloodied bat.

Suderhul, she commanded as she entered the Canary, and shadow bind froze the Bloods in their place. Vitali, an evil mannequin with a bloody bat, followed Kara with his crimson gaze but unless the light and shadow composition of the room changed, such as if the Bloods shone a flashlight or if the candles on the floor burned out, Vitali and his five goons would remain soundless and motionless, bound by their own shadows. Kara didn't have much time before the Bloods in the Priest checked in to see why Vitali had grown silent.

Lucien was a mangled thing on the floor, not an unbroken bone in his body, his jaw dislocated from where the silver bat had struck him on the side of the face, parting his flesh, and the pale cheekbone protruding bare. Whimpering, he curled, pulling up his shattered knee, the frayed jeans soaked in red, when Kara knelt by him and lifted his head. He was shaking wildly.

"Here."

Kara put her wrist to his mouth, but he couldn't bite down and she had to press up into his fangs till her skin and vein pricked. A vampire turned pale from starvation, and feeding on each other made their mind unwell, but Kara had no vampire in her. As far as she knew fae blood wasn't toxic, and other than the missing heart she had her mother's anatomy—the reason most vampires only smelled her human.

It took him a long moment to start sucking softly and swallowing. His mind was unwell with another thing, the den roofies—they'd take some time to clear. But there was no time to wait.

"You need to get up, all right?" said Kara, letting him drink a bit more while she stroked his blood-soaked crown. Because his body was mending itself, bones locking back into place and Lucien finally biting her on his own, she gave him another moment to recover.

They died vile, Kara thought about the fullbloods in Teuf, broken into pieces. Silver, sunlight, and fire, the three deadly things to a vampire, and once their heart or head was gone, there was no coming back from that—they were the Maker's children after all.

"Boss, everything all right?" A voice came from outside the door.

"You have to get up," Kara whispered, and yanked Lucien up.

Not fully conscious, he staggered on his feet. Kara wrapped her arm around his waist and dragged him into the darkness of Teuf. The main entry to Nocturne, the five-mile-long tunnel, probably the way Lucien came in through, was *heavily* guarded. They couldn't go that way. Kara knew other ways out but all of them involved a long hike, some crawling, and travel through pale territories.

An uproar started behind them, Bloods yelling, "Boss! Are you okay, Boss!" They'd figure it out sooner or later. Light and shadow were a common faerie talent, and the ways to counter them were a well-known thing among the vampires.

"Come on," she whispered in the dark, the muck sloshing underneath their feet. "We have to walk a bit faster, Lucien."

"They depended on me to foresee trouble." Lucien's voice faltered, from the injuries probably but she heard grief as well.

"Weep for the dead when we get out of here. In the meantime, get steady on your feet, Pureblood. I can't carry you."

Promise

A good thing about the catacomb was that it was a dark web of tunnels, easy to lose pursuers. A bad thing about the catacomb was that it was a dark web of tunnels, easy to get lost, even if one lived in it for decades.

"How much further?" Lucien asked, spitting blood on the layer of ground-up human bones they were walking on. His body was trying to mend but running around for *seven hours,* according to him, wasn't doing him any favors. "Daylight in an hour, Kara. After that, I can't leave." As he'd said it, his knees folded and he sat down, leaning his back against a wall of stacked skulls.

Passing through the scavengers' quarters back when Kara wasn't lost, she'd bought the speaker from Sebastian for a thousand *dinne* because she hadn't had the time to haggle. She snapped one of her glowsticks to activate it and it turned red. Kneeling on the grey dust that used to be bones, some jagged parts still remaining, Kara held the tube of neon light to Lucien's face.

His pupils were large and black, he was exhausted and verging on fainting. Frowning, he twisted away from the light. "Please don't do that."

The sudden brightness hurt him, Kara thought, and set the glowstick to the side—she needed more light than him.

"Do you have any of your blood vials?" she asked.

"They were in my pocket," said Lucien. "They broke."

"Fine," said Kara, digging through her satchel and lighting her pipe for him. *Krystallis* and not clean blood, but he accepted it, nonetheless.

"Thank you."

Muffled voices and distant footsteps carried through the tunnels like a faint vibration, but Kara couldn't worry about that, maybe they would go another way. Lucien needed a moment of rest. She handed him her baggie to let him smoke whatever he needed.

"Careful about the diamorphine," she warned when he inhaled deeply.

"Yeah," was all he said, closing his eyes.

"Lucien," Kara began, "I promise to get you out of here, but you have to make a promise in kind."

"Whatever you want." Rubbing his thigh and feeling the fabric of his own jeans, his eyelashes fluttering, he chewed his lips. He was feeling the diamorphine.

Kara let him be because she needed to have this conversation *now*. "If I get you out of here, you have to promise me that you'll fix my mind, do what I want, no matter what you see in there. I want to be human."

"I can't make you human," he whispered. He'd said this before. "I can make you *believe* you're human." He'd said that as well.

"That's fine. Do you promise?" she asked because purebloods had a sense of honor, even Vitali, and wouldn't make a promise knowing they wouldn't keep it. Instead of answering, he moaned softly, rolling in his high.

"What are you doing here anyway?" The scarlet eyes half-opened. "You're a faerie, aren't you?"

"Who else have you seen use shadow bind?" Kara asked. "I'll leave you here if you don't promise me. You say it's going to be daylight in an hour. I don't care. That only affects you."

"I saw you hours ahead. You have to tell me why. Was it a faerie trick?"

"I don't know what you're talking about." She checked his forehead. His fever had subsided, and enough time had passed so that his mind should have cleared from the roofie.

"Did you affect my foresight?" He made no sense.

"How did you get here?" Kara asked instead. "Do you have people outside?"

Lucien shook his head. "We flew. I have a Resurgence pilot, but the hangar is some ways from here. I have my car parked just beyond the entrance to the underground, but I can't drive in the daylight."

"Okay, Lucien." Kara got up and held out her hand. "We'll figure it out once we get there, but we have to leave." The voices and the footsteps, now the sound of crushing bones, hadn't faded but were growing louder.

In the faint red glow falling on his face, Lucien tilted his chin up, meeting Kara's gaze but not taking her hand. "Kara, you have to know there are lycans here." He tapped his temple. "I've been hearing them for some time, but I thought they might be pales because I hadn't encountered them before either. I wasn't sure, but now I am. There is a nest of them, pales, right below us, and they sound different."

"If there are lycan in Nocturne..." Kara's voice faded, and they let the implication hang in the still air between them. "How many?" Kara asked about the faerie. Lycans didn't have freewill and didn't travel without their fae master.

"I don't know."

"Is it Whiteswoon?" she asked. Her face went numb.

"I don't know. The fae shield their mind. I can't read them. No Raven can except for Madea." He was honest.

"If it's Whiteswoon, the chances of us getting out of here are none." Kara was honest in return. "If it's someone else, I'll get you out or die trying. But you have to promise me. I want to live as a human. Promise me. Promise me that you'll fix my mind."

"What's wrong with your mind? You seem fine," said Lucien, even as the voices sounded right around the corner. He didn't want to commit to a thing he couldn't honor, which was why Kara trusted him to keep his word.

"When you look into my mind, you will know. But I want your promise now. Make it or I can leave you. They're not looking for me."

"I know."

He was quiet for a while but finally nodded and took her hand, allowing her to pull him up. Kara kicked bone dust over the glowstick, darkness enveloping the corridor, and she let Lucien lead because she couldn't see anything.

It must have been an hour later because Lucien said, "The sun is rising. I can't leave. You should get out of here," while they hid inside an ancient coffin, the owner's brittle bones cracking and collapsing each time Kara moved a little or took a breath.

They were on top of each other, squeezed together and breathing the dust from the dead. A claw scratched the coffin. A pale was right on top of them, whiffling. They moved about on four limbs, occasionally standing erect to see or sniff. Kara had the speaker out of her satchel and clasped in her hand, but she couldn't play it because they'd run into a nest to lose Vitali, Sedric, and about three dozen Bloods stampeding the corridors.

They were so close to the exit that Kara could *sense* the sunlight. Lucien had made her a promise, and given the opportunity he would honor it. Kara may not be pureblood, and she may not have much of anything, never mind honor, but she'd said she'd give it her best shot and she'd meant it. She wouldn't abandon him no matter what time of day it was outside.

The dagger Lucien carried had one edge that was iron for fae, and one edge silver for lycans and vampires. Such a blade was called the *reaper*, she'd learned. As beautifully crafted as the blade was when she gripped the hilt of it, it could not crack a pureblood Blood's marble skin. Only wrought iron, its purest form, was lethal to the fae, not steel, and that was what made the blade brittle. It would snap on Vitali's neck.

"Lycans, Kara," Lucien whispered while she considered her options.

There was a time, long ago, that she'd sought her father's approval, and trained as hard as her human half would hold before collapsing from sheer exhaustion and the mounting injury. But only the Maker knew how long ago that was, not she, and she'd been wasting away in dens for decades at least. She didn't know how much of her training remained, but she was about to find out.

"Here," she whispered in the dark and slipped the hilt of the *reaper* into Lucien's hand. "Should I not come back, don't let the faerie take you alive, you hear? They *will* get what they seek but they won't stop there. They will break you over and over till there is nothing left of you.

If you think Vitali hurt you, you don't know what pain is. If you think you're afraid now, you don't know what fear is. Do you hear?"

She felt his hand tighten around the hilt.

"I won't leave you. If I don't return, I've died," declared Kara, and flung open the lid of the coffin.

The pale that had been standing on it jolted as Kara leaped out, letting the lid drop closed. Naked white shapes glowed like ghosts as she snapped a glowstick and tossed it into the dark. A female pale shrieked, the dark veins visible under her nude white skin, and a gaping hole of black mouth snapped at Kara as she sidestepped, smashing the pale's head against a limestone slab. Its brain matter oozed as its skull broke with a crack. A hundred others tore for her, pale shapes with dark mouths on four limbs. Kara turned on the speaker and a concerto echoed through the hall. Unlike the techno they played at the den, scavengers played classical music because that was what hurt pale ears the most. She stripped off the iron bangles from her wrist and let them drop as well.

The pales scampered from the human sound lost centuries ago, but Vitali's red eyes glowed as the Bloods charged in. The silver bat whooshed and Kara ducked out of the way. The bat striking limestone puffed up grey dust, then glinted from Vitali's fury, a faint light tracing through the air with his swings. Eyes glowed all around Kara, Bloods encircling her. If it was too dark for one to cast a shadow, it was too dark for shadow bind.

He was too slow to hurt her though, and besides, he was swinging with silver. Kara remembered Celeste as she caught his bat. "Would you like to walk in the sun?"

The Blood's eyes swelled, visible in the faint pink of the glowstick. Vitali in her grip, her faerie black claws pierced out of her fingertips and wrapped around the Blood's neck. Kara dragged him through the dark corridors, heading toward where she felt the daylight.

Climbing what may have been a ventilation shaft or a manhole for it had an iron ladder, and lugging Vitali as a spider might carry away its prey, Kara burst out through the metal grating. The tattoo of wings on her back was how she carried her real wings, and the feathers itched for a beat when they unfolded, freed at last from being tucked for so long.

As her grand white wings expanded truly, she soared to the blue skies, the feathers vibrating, absorbing the rays of the rising sun. The free wind whipped Vitali's ponytail into his face as the giant struggled fruitlessly with her. Climbing into the sky soaked with sun, the Blood was catching fire, his screams torn and lost like the fresh flaking of his face. She saw him in the light for the first time and thought he hadn't been that bad looking.

"Goodbye," said she and dropped him from a height enough that he'd burn to cinder before ever hitting the ground. A kind death considering how he lived. He only burned once.

Closing her eyes, she hovered above the clouds, absorbing the sun. Faerie magic came from the light, but if they were angels the Maker must have hated them for he'd made them ugly.

Done with contemplating, she'd keep her promise, and Kara fell back to earth, white clouds and auburn trees passing by, then dove into the mouth of the underground, folding her wings.

Having absorbed the sun, she pulsed with it. *Narnigerel.* A burst of sunlight flashed through the corridors, catching the Bloods and pales on fire. Men with suits and leather jackets, faux from the way they melted onto the skin, burned the same as the pale naked creatures, all flailing black silhouettes in the orange flame.

Meaning to take the coffin and leave Nocturne through the manhole, she dragged the heavy thing through the corridor of dust and bones, but when she tried to push it up through the shaft, it didn't fit. If she could get it erect, she could slide it up the hole, but the layers of bones on the floor were too thick, diminishing the height of the corridor, and it wouldn't angle that way.

More Bloods were coming, howling throughout the tunnels now. She looked up at the foamy white clouds floating on the sea of blue, then down at the screaming dark corridors. She couldn't use sunlight again, not without going out in the daylight. For a beat, she debated if she should go outside and come back in, then decided that would be wasted time—with Lucien around, she couldn't use light anyway.

She pulled the coffin away from the bright spot directly under the shaft and opened the lid. "Come on. We'll find a different way…"

Kara's voice died and she blinked, trying to adjust her sight to the dark. But no matter how hard she rubbed her eyes, the coffin was empty.

Coward

Lucien saw the coffin lid open and a lycan peer in with just enough lead to time bolt from the coffin but be chased by the lycan all the same. Knowing that a lycan was about to grab at his shin wasn't a helpful thing when he was trapped in a tunnel and couldn't crawl any faster. It was experiencing the same fear twice, and a nightmare it was turning out to be.

He didn't know where Kara was or if she was alive. Her death wasn't something he could see even if it was happening now. A Raven foresight triggered only when it affected his immediate surroundings. He couldn't see others' futures, not even for a split second—no one could.

The rocks squeezed him from all sides and his mud-slathered sneakers slipped as Lucien wiggled through a dark hole, hoping it wasn't a dead end, desperate to escape the lycan digging at the tunnel, claws ripping through collapsed slabs to get to him. He'd never seen lycans or faeries before. He wasn't lacking in his knowledge of them, and with all his sparring with Silverfox he'd imagined handling himself far better than he was. For one, he hadn't thought he was a coward, but here he was, running as cowards did.

Grunting, he climbed out of the hole and dropped into a flooded room. If there used to be a way out, it was submerged, and sloshing around in the pitch dark he couldn't see shit. Running like a dog chasing his tail, Lucien was getting his mind into a frenzy and the dark wasn't helping.

He heard the lycan rise from the water before it did and drew his *reaper,* the only thing he could do, because it was a dead end. He couldn't run anymore. The blade stuck to the wet scabbard coming out, but it was bare in his hand when the dark water bubbled, dripping as a monster rose from it in front of him. A set of red eyes glared as a low growl vibrated through the air. He swung but something yanked and the scream never left his throat—he felt that twice. Swallowing dirty water, he got dragged through it. So, not one lycan but two. Kicking and flailing, he lost all orientation. Unlike dipping in the lake, no golden moon or bright constellations called him to the surface. All was dark. To keep his sanity, to know what was real and what was an echo, he suppressed his Raven sight.

Finding himself kneeling, coughing out filthy water, he blinked, his eyes adjusting to the light. Some candles were lit on the ground. From what he knew, the fae didn't see all that well in the dark, and there was one in the room. He was glad to not have seen that twice so he could only be scared once.

In front of a wall of stacked skulls, faces of the dead with black sockets for eyes and nose, the faerie with long white hair, ghostly as if he never walked in the sun, stood wearing his large wings draped around himself like a feathery cloak. He had a perfectly symmetrical face even as he arched one eyebrow, and he'd hiked up his long black velvet robe so as not to brush the gold trimmed hem on dirt, revealing elegant boots. A tall collar with gold embroidery cupped the sides of his slender neck, and Lucien wouldn't have thought such a graceful creature to be cruel and vile had he not known better.

"What is your name, young one?" asked the faerie, his mouth black when he opened it, and eyes a set of mirrors into the void that didn't reflect the candlelight in the room.

Lucien tried to rise but a lycan claw pressed down on his shoulder, bringing him to his knees again. He spat some dirt or bone dust that had gotten lodged behind his molars while he was being dragged through the muck.

"What is your name?" asked the fae again.

Lucien didn't answer. They must already know who he was. Vitali had allowed a faerie into his city. The Bloods had broken covenant and he assumed their betrayal was complete. Anything the Bloods knew, surely this creature did as well.

"He doesn't speak, Master. Perhaps he doesn't have a tongue. Should I check?" A lycan, one of the three in the room, came around Lucien and bent, bringing his face a breath away from him.

Enormous wolves with red eyes and double rows of dentition, they stood on their hindlegs but ran on all four. Their thick black fur was sharp like porcupine quills and prickled up when they were irritated and shot like darts if they were attacked. Nearly impossible to penetrate the heart, lycans had two sets of ribcages.

'Set them on fire. Go for the neck, and don't forget your shield,' Silverfox used to say. *'And remember, they are both faster and stronger than you, so keep your distance and use your gift. And whatever you do, do not confront a lycan in the presence of his master. In close proximity, the faerie can suppress your ability to predict, and without it, you can't hope to win.'*

"Child," said the faerie, the feathery cloak parting as he towered over Lucien on his knees. A velvet sleeved pale arm reached out, the clawed hand tipping his chin up with a finger. "How far into the future can Madea see? What are her plans for the Longdark? These two questions you will answer and show me *all* of Resurgence's defenses before you may ask me for the mercy of death. How long you wish to suffer is wholly up to you."

Shamefully, Lucien had lost his blade being dragged through the water, and his bare hands clenched as a lycan pulled his arms over his head, slamming him onto the limestone floor underneath the layer of dust.

Like a giant white moth, the fae wings fluttered over him, before the creature knelt on his chest and touched his crown with his cold bony hand, the claws digging into his scalp when he grabbed. Lucien kicked, his heels scuffing on the ground when the faerie gutted him with silver. He ground his teeth, his breathing stuttering as he tried to control the pain of the silver blade twisting inside him. He could hear the cutting and it sounded like the butcher's shop. *It's not so bad,* he convinced himself. Pretending a hurt didn't hurt—he was well adept at it.

The last time something had hurt was when he was seven and Francis kicked him and broke three of his ribs. He sniveled about it to his mother, and Madea slapped him across the face for lying. He complained to his father about the whole thing and Silverfox was enraged. The Ravens were at each other's throats for weeks, during which Lucien had learned that Francis's men outnumbered Silverfox's three to one. The ordeal ended with Nana, the woman who used to care for Lucien, 'slipping' and falling down the keep's stairs. She'd been human and had broken her back. After that, nothing hurt.

It didn't hurt getting flogged for being a brat when he was eleven. It had been Christmas, a human girl had invited him home and he wanted to go instead of standing on guard duty outside Madea's bedchamber. It didn't hurt being asked to *weave* awful things, and it didn't hurt when he overheard Silverfox speaking with Madea, saying, *'What do I care for the child? He's ungifted and weak. I love you only, my Queen.'*

He tried not to fault his father for always taking her side because he was bonded to her. Yet, she'd rejected him, it was plain to see. Lucien suspected Madea had bonded with her own brother, Francis, and the charade with Silverfox was for appearance only. So, there was that, and that didn't hurt either.

"What were my two questions, child? Do you remember?" he heard the faerie ask. The small pale face with sharp features and dark eyes was a blur because of the tears welling in his eyes—an involuntary reflex. The burn wasn't so bad.

"Fuck you." When he breathed, blood sprayed the faerie's face. The knife was in his lungs.

Of the three things the faerie had wanted: the queen's plan during the eclipse, the length of the queen's foresight, and knowledge of the Resurgence's defenses, two of those didn't matter and were probably a test. One, Madea was going to attack Groom Lake, Whiteswoon's base of power, during the eclipse—even Vitali could guess at that. Two, Lucien didn't know jack about Resurgence's defenses. He wasn't one of the officers. So, there was only one question really, Madea's Raven sight.

A secret, even among Ravens, not everyone knew the correct answer. But unfortunately, Lucien did because Silverfox did. Two hours and fifteen minutes precisely was how far Madea could foresee her own future. When she was on the battlefield as she used to be during the Bloodline War, it was an advantage even Whiteswoon couldn't overcome. No one could ambush her. Nothing could surprise her, and she'd *always* won despite incredible odds—but that was when her mind was well. Such a queen, Lucien had never seen. Yet, he couldn't tip the greatest advantage the Ravens, therefore Resurgence—hundreds of thousands of lives—had. So, this was how he died. Being cut to pieces by a faerie in a filthy dark hole far away from home. Oh well, it wasn't so bad.

"Vamperish immortalis!" he defiantly yelled when the faerie pulled the blade out.

"Is it pride, Pureblood?" asked the faerie, standing over him and cocking his head to the side. "If it's pride that binds your tongue, I can relieve you of it. Are you asking me to humiliate you? Because I can."

"Fuck you."

"Careful, child. Keep asking for it and my lycans may oblige you," said the faerie. "What is the human expression?" He knotted his pale brows as if trying to recall, then asked, "Is it 'knock on the devil's door long enough, and eventually, someone will answer you?' That's it, isn't it?"

"Right you are, Master," said a lycan. "Would you like me to get the door?"

The faerie tapped his chin. "I don't want to be ugly. The faerie folk aren't ugly, it's you who make us so."

The lycans, or at least one of them, was male, apparently. Lucien kicked it when it grabbed him, his knee connecting with a large squishy cock that had been hidden inside the fur. Not so hidden, a raw red tip slid out like an aroused dog. Lucien scrambled to get away from it.

It grabbed him and yanked, hauling him through the dirt. Lucien wheezed breathlessly when its claws skewered through his back, right through his lungs, and bolted him to the ground. He couldn't turn, the lycan's weight was on him. *It's not so bad, it wouldn't hurt,* he was thinking when the weight lifted off him and he could breathe—the claws that pinned him were gone as well. He tried to get up, staggered, fell, then on hands and knees he crawled to a dark corner and folded into himself, pulling his knees to his chest.

Things were screeching and he didn't want to look. Pales, lycans, faeries—he'd seen enough for the day and just wanted a moment's break.

A nursery rhyme about an old man looped in his head. A thing Nana used to make him repeat to calm him down.

Knick-knack paddy whack, he was counting in his head and was up to five when he heard Kara. "Are you all right?"

He lifted his head from his knees and saw that she had wings. The feathers were pulsing with soft light, not too hard on his eyes. She was holding two blades, larger versions of the tattoos she had on the arms—which were gone. They had a chain attached to the hilt which was wrapped around her arms and he thought she must throw them during a fight. The wings, the swords, they weren't ink but things she carried. She flicked the blood from her blades and wiped them on her naked thigh. When the blades dissipated like smoke, her tattoos reappeared.

"Here." She held out her hand and he took it but flinched when her wings moved. She stowed them away then. They lay on her back and became traces of ink again.

"Good news. That wasn't Whiteswoon." She pointed at the faerie head on the ground. The lycans were diced in chunks and looked like a mound of mush. "Bad news. I've killed Vitali and now they know I'm a faerie."

"Okay," was all Lucien said.

"Are you all right?" She frowned.

"No."

Premonition

In a dark room, a passageway between two tunnels partially collapsed, the walls were full of graffiti, expressions of humans dead centuries long. Lucien and Kara sat on a stone ledge next to each other. Kara snapped a stick and tossed it on the ground and it glowed pink.

"That's the last one," she said.

Lucien checked the time. "It's six in the evening. Two hours till sunset," he said.

It only affected him, of course, because the faerie walked in the light, but Kara hadn't left him. Instead, she sat surrounded by spray paintings of a nude woman, a marijuana leaf, a white skull on a dark banner, a two foot tall cock depicted to be ejaculating, and names and words of the dead.

After sharing her *krystallis* with him, which Lucien was beginning to appreciate the dulling effect of, she got up and went to a wall with a red heart. Two names were written inside with white paint and connected with a plus sign.

"What does it feel like?" she asked, tracing the heart with her finger.

"What?" Lucien asked, exhaling red mist in the pink glow, letting the diamorphine take the edge off.

"To have a beating heart."

"That's not what one looks like," said Lucien about the cartoon heart.

"I know that," Kara said. "But it's drawn like this, with two arches, because it's two hearts together, signifying love, no?"

He didn't know and shrugged but Kara with her back turned to him didn't see. "Are you asking about heart or love?" he asked.

"Both, I suppose. To have a heart is to love, isn't it?"

"Everyone has a heart," said Lucien forgetting momentarily that the faerie did not. "But not everyone loves. So, I suppose not."

"That's a shame," said Kara, turning. "I want to have a heart that beats."

"Have you seen The Wizard of Emerald City?"

"Emerald City?" She frowned, perhaps trying to remember such a place.

"It's a book, and also a film. I have both in my room. I'll show it to you some time."

"Where do you live?"

"Raven Keep..." Lucien looked down at the grey dust in the pink glow. "Thank you."

"What for?" She came and sat by him again.

"For not leaving me."

"I promised," she said. "You're very young, aren't you? How old are you?"

"Twenty-four."

"Years old? You're the youngest vampire I've ever met."

"How old are you?" he asked.

"I was born at the end of the war."

"So, like a hundred? That's not very old," he said.

"It's been that long since the war ended?"

"The war never ended, not really," said Lucien. "But yeah, it's been a hundred years since the last large scale military operation against the faerie."

Across from Lucien, there was a drawing of a skeleton with a bowtie giving a speech from a podium and he'd been staring at it, wondering what he might be saying, when Kara turned to him and asked, "Do you think I'm revolting?"

"No." Inadvertently, he flicked a gaze at her back. Knowing that they were real wings was disturbing, but other than that... no.

"It's okay if you do. I'm just asking."

"No, I thought you were beautiful when I first saw you. That hasn't changed. Wouldn't have even if you hadn't saved my life twice."

"You're strange," she said, kicking off her tennis shoes. She was even shorter now that she wasn't wearing heels. "Your clothes are ruined." Looking down, she patted his knee where he'd scabbed it. The injury was gone but the tear and the bloodstain remained. "This too." She pinched his T-shirt, more red and grey than white.

"I have more clothes. It's okay."

The faerie had lifted his shirt to carve him up, so the injury was mostly underneath. But that would heal in a while, and it won't be cumbersome to move around. The time he'd pulled out his fangs had taken the longest to heal, but physical injuries, other than from the sun, healed completely within hours. So, it wasn't so bad.

He'd been thinking that when Kara stroked his hair, then her hand slid down to pat his back. "Don't be so sad. I'll get you out here. You'll be going home soon." She smiled.

"I'm not sad."

"You're not a good liar. I'm not either, so that's good." She scooted away a bit, then tapped her thigh. "Lay your head here. It's better than the rocks. Sleep a little. Vampires need sleep. Give me your watch and I'll keep track of time for you."

He was exhausted, so he lay down, putting his head in her lap. She glided her fingers through his hair and it was pleasant. He took off his watch and handed it to her. Foolishly, he attempted to instruct her how to tell time, but she laughed.

"I know how to read the clock," she said. "Just like I can read the four-letter word, love. All right, sleep for an hour, it says it's nearly seven now."

"People in Nocturne wear a lot of glitter and shine," mused Lucien when Kara adjusted her position and the sequins of her dress rustled.

"We live in the dark but like to be seen." She hadn't been adjusting but digging through her satchel, and from it, she handed him a small thing. It was a porcelain heart with 'Be Happy' written on it.

"You can have it," she said.

"I already have the pillow one." He slid his hand into his pocket to look for it. "Oh, I lost it. It's gone."

"It's okay, now you have this one. It's better."

"Thank you," he said, weighing the tiny heart on his palm, hoping not to lose or break it. "How far is the exit, do you know?"

"About three miles," she said. "It's better to wait here till you're sure it's dark outside... in case we run into more trouble."

"Right."

Settling into Kara's lap, he closed his eyes. He was *so* tired. For someone who had very little trust, he was extending all of it to her. But what other options did he have? If they managed to get out of Nocturne he still had to drive back to the hangar. Sean wouldn't leave him, but the faeries could have found and killed him by now.

"Kara, can you fly a plane?" he asked because he couldn't.

"No, but I can fly. I can carry you. Is that what you're asking?"

No, that hadn't been it. He was too tired to answer and was already falling asleep.

'They're just boys,' the queen had said about Vitali and Sedric. *Just go tell them I'm calling, that is all. You* can *do that, right?'* Her crimson eyes narrowed, her midnight hair jarring against her pale complexion, a side of her face discolored and cracked like a broken porcelain mask. Supposedly, she'd walked out in the sun once and had scars all over.

Why, he thought. Not about Madea's sun walk, but about Kara. He'd seen her hours ahead. Had he not foreseen her standing in that hall, selling a yarn heart, he would have left Nocturne before dawn and wouldn't have met her—his vision had self-fulfilled and that wasn't how Raven sight worked. Raven foresight didn't cause itself. Predicting a cup falling, moving to catch it, then accidentally knocking it and making it fall, whereas otherwise it wouldn't have, *wasn't* how Raven sight worked. His bloodline talent didn't take itself into consideration. The cup would have fallen whether he'd foreseen it or not.

Yet, his sight had caused him to meet Kara, and that was something completely different: a premonition. Sometimes, Raven elders gifted with sight—not all were—had premonitions far into the future about the most significant event of their life. Madea had predicted the Long-dark *years* ago. A month ago, Francis had a premonition about his victory at Groom Lake, or so he'd proclaimed. And he'd been certain that it had been during the eclipse.

'The sun was high in the sky, but it was black,' he said, giving a grand sermon. *'And with this hand, I've held Whiteswoon's severed head.'*

Silverfox hadn't contested it, but he wasn't gifted with foresight. His art was in *weaving,* and he could speak telepathically.

Not asleep, not awake, Lucien had been drifting when he heard Kara. "Let's get out of here, yeah?"

He was so tired, so fucken tired, that Kara had to pull him up.

Two

Demon

The five decades of the Bloodline War decimated the human cities and nature had reclaimed it in the century since. Out through the roof of an apartment complex skeleton, paint chipped pillars with broken windows dark in the moonlight, an enormous tree had grown, an explosion of rustling leaves. A ravine flowed through the jagged earth, splitting a parking lot. The streets existing a few feet at a time in the headlights were covered in green moss, and the signs as well. The upholstery in Lucien's black car was genuine leather, and Kara rolled down the windows as a slow, nagging rain began tapping the windshield. The air smelled of damp earth and the outside world was beautiful.

Despite the rain, the night wasn't dark. A pale light, the moon through a break in the clouds, was falling on Lucien's profile as Kara observed him.

"Do you mind if I put my feet up on the seat?" she asked because his things were so nice and she didn't want to ruin them. But they'd been driving for some time and not used to sitting in a car, her back was beginning to ache.

"Sure," he said. "Do as you like."

On the dark road, rusted cars partially covered in ivy passed by on both sides, ruins too, and the leaves occasionally blowing by the headlights were orange and auburn. *It's fall,* she thought, the concept of seasons beyond just the flood level of Nocturne returning to her slowly.

Lucien had left his car some ways from the entrance to Nocturne, inside a partially collapsed structure, covered with branches and shrubs. Once they were outside he had no trouble finding it, but they'd walked for a long time to get to it.

"How long does the night last?" Kara asked.

"We're going to be barely making it," he said, cursing under his breath. "The rain isn't helping."

Lycans and Bloods both could track through rain and mud, and they couldn't spend another day in the vicinity. Sedric would be out for her to avenge his brother, and the faerie would be coming as well once they learned one of theirs didn't return.

"What did they want from you? The faerie, I mean," Kara asked.

The way he pursed his lips, he wasn't going to answer. That was fine. Kara held out her arm through the open window, feeling the cool, soft spray. Perhaps it was the *krystallis*, or perhaps everything in the world was beautiful, including the boy sitting beside her.

"I'm glad to have met you," she said. "Even if it doesn't work out and we die here tonight."

He flicked a look at her just then, his expression unreadable. "We're not going to die here," he said, the scarlet gaze returning to the road. "I'll take you to the Resurgence as I've promised. I'll try and mend your mind as I've promised."

Wings beat above them and they both tensed, but it was an owl diving in the headlight and snatching a small thing, probably a mouse, from the road and flying off.

Kara reached for his hand that was on the steering wheel, and he let go of it to lace his fingers with hers, his other hand taking the wheel.

"Say something to me," he said. "I'm spent. I might fall asleep."

"Something." She smiled, thinking she should let go of his hand because it was becoming strange, but not doing it because the strange felt good. "I want to remember you. Will I?" She was being silly asking it, but her consciousness spanning a century fought to live, to remain, and it wanted her to remember things such as that she liked hearts and this moment.

"You will know who I am. The Resurgence is friendly with Ravens, but beyond that, probably not," he said, letting go of her hand. "Had you always been human, you would have never been at Nocturne. And that's how that works. Your memories make sense in relation to each other. If I miss something, if you recall something out of place, your mind tries to solve it and will obsess over it, trying to make sense of the thing that doesn't. So, you were never here and would have never met me, not in a den called Priest anyway."

Kara let that sink in. Then, she pressed her hand on her chest because it felt like an ache, but she wasn't injured. So she let it go.

The wipers swiped rhythmically as the sky hung heavy with thick, dark clouds. A thunderstorm was brewing.

"Should you still be driving?" Kara asked, flicking a look at the brightening horizon despite the charged weather.

"We're almost there," said Lucien, the engine howling and the car flying.

In the greying light, she saw that the loose locks coming down to his earlobes had not only chestnut brown but were mixed with a lighter color like gold and caramel, and his irises were the bright red of fresh blood. The knuckles of his hand gripping the wheel had turned white. His T-shirt was dirtied by dust and mud from the catacomb. Blood stains where Vitali had beaten him and the faerie had tortured him had darkened to maroon.

He shot her a questioning look and she realized she'd been staring at him. "What?" he asked.

"These will scar," she said.

"It's not that bad," he said.

"I didn't mean just your body."

"I know what you meant. I'm fine," he said.

"Does it hurt?"

"No." He was a liar.

Kara sighed. "My mind is ugly. I don't want to make yours as well. Is there no way to dump the memories without you having to take them on?"

He looked at her for a beat before returning his gaze to the road. "I'm not taking them as you say, but I do have to see what I'm doing."

"My father is Whiteswoon," said Kara expecting a big reaction but Lucien didn't flinch, and the engine didn't miss a beat. "Does that matter?"

"My mother is Madea. Do you know who she is?"

"The Fae Slayer," said Kara.

"No, that's Gabriela Arriaga. Madea is the Raven Queen. My mother and your father are mortal enemies. Does that matter?"

"No."

"Then, I guess it doesn't," he said. "We're not them."

What a kind thing to say, thought Kara. Someone knowingly and purposefully told her she wasn't her father.

Among the old oaks, a great metal wheel leaning to the side passed by the window. Gasping, Kara pointed at it. Painted in the colors of a faded rainbow, the thing had been beautiful. Perhaps it was the Maker's wheel that he drove the earth with.

"What is that?" she exclaimed.

Lucien flicked a look in the rearview mirror, then said, "Ferris Wheel."

"Faerie's Wheel?"

"No, Ferris. We're passing by an old amusement park."

A park that amuses? Kara felt the corners of her mouth tugging upward at the silly concept. "How does a park amuse?"

"Do you know what a fair is?"

"No."

"Well, then you're in luck. You're just in time for the Fall Fair," he said, pressed a knob on the panel of the car, and music flooded the cabin.

Unlike the techno beat of the den, the music had a piano and a man sang playfully as if he was laughing. *Meet me in St. Louis, Louis,* he sang, taking Kara's breath away. The man sang that he'd come home, but his wife wasn't there. She'd left a note, telling him to meet her at the state fair.

"Is it a place with bright lights?" Kara asked about the fair.

"And a Ferris Wheel." Although he was trying to keep his composure and putting on music to distract himself, Kara saw the faint light was hurting him. Hissing, he was gritting his teeth.

"Lucien, stop it. It's not worth it."

"We can make it," he gritted, turning the music up louder.

"Why don't mosquitoes bite vampires?" She asked an old joke from the den to distract him from the pain.

"Our blood is toxic."

That hadn't been the joke, but Kara let it go. He wasn't in the mood to be laughing anyway.

Another song came on and a woman sang as lightning thundered across the grey sky like a silver whip.

I feel so lonely

Just for you only...

If you say we can make it, I believe you, thought Kara. As it turned out, she would believe him about anything, because she wanted him to say that she was human, had a heart, and wasn't ugly or evil—and believe it.

Through a clearing in the trees emerged the largest shed Kara had ever seen, earth colored and hidden amongst the shrubs, its wide door open like a gaping mouth. A man in a green uniform sprinted out of the shed toward them, carrying a folded tarp.

He was yelling, the words lost in the roar of the engine, the rain and the wind lashing at the windshield, but as Lucien pulled a lever, throwing the car into a skid, the man yanked the driver's door open.

He covered Lucien with the tarp and shoved him aside on top of Kara, yelling, "Are you fucken insane?"

The door slammed, the man mumbling a curse, and Kara felt the car move. Under the black tarp with Lucien, him on top of her and squeezed together on the same seat, she didn't see him but felt his soaring fever. His skin was hot to the touch like holding her hand above a burning candle.

When he'd said, *'It's fine, I'm fine,'* and kept on driving, he'd lied. He'd nearly caught the sun's flames.

The human, the man with the green uniform and the tarp, continued to berate Lucien for his 'insanity' as he helped him up the ladder into an airplane. They were inside the shed, 'Hangar 37' spray painted on the wall.

"Where are the others?" he was asking.

"It's just us, Sean," said Lucien, his arm draped around the human bearing most of his weight as they climbed the ladder. "Faerie on our tail, take off immediately."

"Fuck," Sean hissed, and looked back at Kara over his shoulder. "What is she?"

Lucien answered but she didn't hear him. Lightning flashed and thunder boomed, then they disappeared into the airplane leaving Kara standing alone in the shed, unsure of what to do. Was she supposed to follow them in? Lucien hadn't said so.

As soon as she took a step onto the ladder Sean came out running, his black boots with laces drumming the metal steps.

"Human?" he yelled on his way down. He was a man with deep creases of concern around his eyes and greying short hair showing from under his green cap. His beard also had some grey. "Welcome to the Resurgence." He strode past her. "I need to pull the Jag into cargo. You go outside, strip the camo off the runway, all right?"

Kara understood 'outside', and because Sean glared at her, Kara ran outside, then spun around, getting soaked, and wiping her face to be able to see in the pouring rain.

She was still fumbling around when Sean came out and they peeled off a rubber netting covering a paved road, and once she understood what he'd meant, she rolled it and hauled it into the hangar by herself.

"Do you wrestle or something?" Sean asked in wonderment once they were inside the hangar.

"No, I fight," Kara said.

"Even better." He gave her the thumbs up.

When his back turned to her, she tried the 'thumbs up' expression herself. It was a human thing to do.

They climbed up the ladder, the thing beginning to fold itself up with a mechanical whirring sound as they entered the plane. Lucien was on one of the seats at the back, but she didn't get to ask him if he was all right or to enjoy the scent of all the genuine leather in the cabin before she was pulled through a door at the front, Sean locking the latch behind them.

The cabin had a wide window, and two grey seats jammed inside screens and panels. But unlike the junk the scavengers collected, opening and tinkering with the wires to sometimes get them working, all the screens were unbroken, coming alive as Sean hopped into the seat to the left and began flipping switches.

"Come on, girl, it ain't the museum. Take a seat and strap on."

Careful not to touch anything, Kara stepped over the panels and settled into the empty seat.

"Have you seen it? The faerie?" asked Sean, steering the plane out of the hangar, and the pouring rain immediately drummed the metal roof and blurred the windows.

Kara didn't know how to answer that and shrugged, but Sean kept on talking to himself.

"The fuckers haven't crossed the Atlantic in a century. The end game is truly upon us with the Longdark, I suppose... All right, take note, girl," he said. "You're my lookout. Keep your eyes peeled for faerie."

The plane straightened on the runway, paused, then lunged forward with the sound of a hurricane caught in a tunnel, vibrating, screaming, gathering more and more speed. She winced, thinking they were going to crash right into the trees, but the nose tilted up with a feeling of someone pressing down on Kara.

"Hold on, girl," Sean yelled, but Kara wasn't sure if he was speaking to her or his plane. "Steep climb!"

The heaviness, the hand pressing on Kara lightened, but all she saw was grey as they climbed toward the sky. Remembering she should be looking out for faerie, she tried not to be overwhelmed with the strangeness of it all. She'd seen the sky. She could fly. But not like this. The wind and rain not whipping her hair into her face, she could actually see the Maker's home—heaven.

"Fifteen hundred feet!" Sean called out. "Get sharp!"

The plane shook. Kara's fear was not that the metal tube would snap and that she'd fall through the sky, but that should the metal tube snap, it was daylight outside. Her mind was on the vampire in the cabin.

"Five thousand feet!"

They were passing through the clouds, and at this rate there was no way to see a faerie until he was on the windshield, but rotating her head aimlessly, Kara scanned as best as she could.

"Sixty-five hundred!"

"I don't know what that means!" Kara yelled back.

"The faerie need to breathe! Twenty-six thousand is their ceiling, all right?"

She nodded as if Sean was looking at her, he wasn't. "At what height do the planes fly?" she yelled.

"We'll reach flight altitude at thirty-five thousand! Hold on!"

Then Kara understood; the plane was only vulnerable during its climb and at descent, but once it reached its flight path most faeries couldn't touch it—that was some relief. But it was debatable if Whiteswoon *needed* to breathe. He inhaled and exhaled, his chest moving when he did so, but the lack of air wouldn't kill him. That was true of vampires as well. They breathed, yet choking wasn't how they silvered each other.

When Sean called, "Eight thousand," the plane's nose pierced out of the cloud, shooting up in the crystal blue sky. The sun on its east horizon was on their tail, and Kara soaked in the endless blue without any glare on the window.

"The Maker lives here," she whispered too quiet for Sean to hear her. All her ink, the twin blades on her arms and the wings on her back, pulsed with power. Perhaps it was true that the faerie were once angels like the human depictions, men with feathered wings. The images predated the faerie arrival by a millennium... Yet, had it been ever true that they were once children of the Maker, they'd fallen far, far from grace, a long, long time ago.

That makes you a demon, doesn't it, Father?

Mother

After Sean made an announcement about having reached a safe altitude and the flight time being two and a half hours, Lucien's voice came over the speaker asking to see Sean.

"Can the plane fly itself?" asked Kara, worried, as Sean unbuckled his seatbelt and rose.

"Sure." He pressed a button and an orange light, 'Autopilot engaged', came on with a ding.

"Is there a bathroom?" asked Kara, getting up as well. She wanted to smoke.

"Sure." Sean motioned for her to follow, then pressed a button by the door and spoke into it. "Light, Lucien," he warned before opening the door.

Black shutters were pulled over the round windows on the sides of the plane, but a row of soft yellow light glowed from the curved ceiling of the cylinder-shaped cabin. Grey genuine leather seats large enough for two lined the two sides of the cabin, and the beige carpet was so clean that

Kara took off her shoes to walk on the aisle. The fabric was soft under her feet.

Lucien was in one of the foremost seats, leaning back a little as he said, "Take a seat," to Sean.

Sean sat down across the aisle from Lucien. Initially, Kara had waited because she didn't see where the bathroom was. Also, she'd wanted to ask if Lucien needed *Krystallis*—he'd nearly burned. Then she realized she didn't want to be eavesdropping and asked for the bathroom.

Both men pointed at the door marked 'lavatory'.

The lavatory was a tiny space with a metal sink and a toilet bowl. She latched the door, then summoned fire on her palm to heat the shards in the glass bowl. There were no candles around and she never got her lighter fixed.

Light, shadow, fire which was channeled sunlight, and glamour or mind control were four arts of faerie. Of those four, glamour was high art—only some faerie could trick the mind, and Whiteswoon was the master of it. Being a halfblood, Kara had no glamour, and that was the only good thing about her. At least she didn't have the temptation to use the vilest of magic.

She gripped the rim of the metal sink as the diamorphine rushed through her. Star and Eshe flickered through her mind as shadows when she closed her eyes. *Be well.* She thought of them, of how beautiful Eshe was when she laughed, her bronze skin glistening in the candlelight. She recalled how 'bitch' was a term of endearment Star used, flipping his long, blue hair. His manicure was always perfect. She thought of Sebastian the scavenger, the only man to think her pretty. A man who was going to die during the Longdark, following a dream he had of freedom—Lyon.

The Longdark had first started as a rumor along the fringes, then at some point it turned into a fact—a thing everyone took for truth. No one knew how they knew or why it was happening. They just believed it with absolute certainty such as the leaves changing color in the fall.

The door opened, and it was Lucien. "Are you all right?" he asked.

"A man gave me many hearts, and I left him. Am I evil?" Kara was high, swaying back and forth.

"A man has only one heart," said Lucien, stepping into the tight space with her.

She extended her pipe to him, which he took. *Gal*—she ignited a flame on her palm for him.

"Have you ever loved?" she asked.

"For a Raven to love is to bond, and we do that only once in our life. So, no."

"I loved my mother, but she didn't love me," Kara said. "I suppose my one love is spent."

"You're not a Raven." Lucien exhaled red mist, his breath close in the confined space.

"Can't love anyway because I don't have a heart," Kara said. "It just felt as if I loved her because her death hurt. That's what hearts do, isn't it? They hurt."

"They often do," said Lucien, reaching over to wipe a hair from her face and tucking it behind her ear. "Come on out. I told Sean you're human. You can trust him, but don't do this around him." He held her hand that she'd ignited flame with.

"Does that mean I can't smoke *krystallis* now?"

"Sure, you can. Plenty of humans indulge in diamorphine. Just don't use magic is all I'm saying."

Kara nodded.

They exited the lavatory together, then they shared a seat. Lucien got a light wool blanket from the overhead compartment, leaned the seat back like a bed, and covered them both. The blanket smelled of open field, lavender, and sunlight. Sean was flying the plane and it was only the two of them in the cabin.

"Lucien," she whispered and laid her head on his chest. He had a strong heart that beat rhythmically, and she tried not to compare it to the metronome on Whiteswoon's grand piano. "I didn't expect you to take me home. You could have altered my memory and left me anywhere."

"You said you wanted to be happy, and you can't do that alone. Humans live together and Resurgence is the only safe place I know."

She considered it, then said, "I'm glad to have met you." Then she closed her eyes and began drifting to sleep for the first time in a *long* time.

His arm around her shoulder tightened in an embrace. "Me too."

The flight was too short and their time together too brief. Kara thought she'd only closed her eyes, but Sean was already announcing the descent over the speakers. Groaning, Kara rose, thinking to look out for the faerie, but Lucien pulled her back down.

"Don't worry about it. We're entering controlled airspace." He'd been asleep as well and his voice was raspy. "I have to put you in luggage and haul you out. The fewer people see you, the fewer favors I'll owe."

I'd hate to not remember you, Kara thought, falling asleep despite the loud and vibrating plane. No one had held her before and she wanted to stay like this, in his embrace, for as long as she could.

They'd landed in Greenwillow, Raven County. The Resurgence was in Summerset, a neighboring prefecture as explained by Lucien.

Lucien had her lie down in a tin box, the wheels rattling as he pulled it. There were many voices, but when the lid opened Lucien and she were at the back of a truck without any windows. He pressed his index finger over his lips and mouthed, "It's a few hours' drive."

At late dusk, light failing and giving way to black, Kara stood barefoot on autumn grass. The ocean was grey and breaking against the cliff with a hiss and thunder as the weather began spritzing a mist of cool water.

The two-story white limestone cottage with a sloping thatched roof had some vegetation growing around it and a redheaded woman with puffy hair and a girl who looked just like her mother came out to greet them. Sean's family, Kara realized, as the pilot, now the driver, stepped out of the van and the girl ran to him, screaming, "Papa!"

She wasn't the first child Kara had seen, for the faerie kept human servants and they had children, but she was the first happy child she'd seen.

Sean's wife exchanged words with Lucien which were lost in the spray of the ocean before reaching Kara's ears. The night draft rustled through the tall grass, and Kara running her fingertips over it felt the dew—the world was an infinitely splendid place fleeting away with each passing moment, giving way to another. She didn't doubt that the morning would be striking as the sun rose over the cliffs, but the moments of her life that contained Lucien were depleting and she savored each one as they passed her by.

She was invited to have supper with the Doyles—that was Sean's last name, and both his wife and daughter carried it—and her jaw muscles practiced a forgotten motion of chewing. The faerie ate human food as well as human flesh and were particularly fond of sour green apples and raw red hearts. Being fall, the Doyles had apples, but their lamb was cooked. Kara couldn't eat bread because dough made the faerie ill, but everything else she sampled.

Lucien sat at the table with them but didn't eat. He drank whiskey and played a game of flicking bone bits with Riona, the little girl, whom he seemed to know well. After dinner, Sean's wife who was called Eilis, drew blood from Lucien with an ivy, pooling it into a plastic pouch. She gave a spoonful to Riona, calling it 'medicine', then stored the rest in the refrigerator they had in the kitchen corner.

"Riona has bone cancer," Lucien explained later as he and Kara were looking at the constellation on the porch, sharing a bowl of *krystallis.* "She's too young to be turned but my blood keeps her illness at bay. Sean's loyalty to me is absolute. So don't worry, I'm leaving you with people I trust. They'll look after you well."

"You don't trust him enough to tell him about me?" she asked. She was thankful for what he was doing but her concern was that she might be endangering a little girl.

"That's not a matter of trust," said Lucien. "He'd think I've lost my mind. He'd think I'm being glamoured and to help me, he'd report it. I know him."

The Doyles had gone to sleep, but the tankard of ale Sean had left out sat between Lucien and Kara. Wanting to try it, Kara reached for it but Lucien said, "Bread and beer use the same yeast. Maybe don't drink it if bread makes you sick."

"Oh." Kara retracted her hand.

"Here." He gave her his glass of whiskey. "It's rare we get clear sky like this in the fall. It will probably rain in the morning." He pointed at the hills, jagged dark shapes on the horizon. The ocean was to their back, constantly hissing then withdrawing like a great lung breathing. "If it does, watch the fog. I've never seen it in the light but I imagine it's serene, the thick white rolling through the gold and auburn trees."

"Do you see the full spectrum of colors?" Kara asked. "The shades of fall are a splendid variety in the light, but at night, it's mostly black."

"I've seen daylight in the films. I love them. I read them in the books as well, and I can imagine the colors. But you're right, it's mostly black at night. Sometimes I wonder why the creator made us this way. Sunlight gives life to all but kills us."

"Those who live in the light age and die. It's a give and take, I suppose."

"Not the faerie, though."

"No, not the faerie." Kara sighed. "I wish they did. I loathe them... what happens when I live with humans and they notice I don't... age?"

"That's at least a decade away, or maybe even two. I'll figure out something by then." Lucien turned to her with a smile. Then he traced his finger through the sky and said, "The Big Dipper, and that's Polaris. It's always in the north, in case you get lost."

"I don't get lost."

"Must be nice."

"Lucien?"

"Yeah?"

Do you want to be with me? she wanted to ask but he'd already said no, so she shrugged, and instead said, "The bonding, how does that work? The Bloods don't bond."

"Yeah, it's something specific to Raven purebloods. When we're intimate with our mate, we fall in love forever."

"Why?"

"I don't know."

"Are your parents bonded?"

"No."

Kara frowned because she didn't understand. 'Being intimate' was an odd way of saying fucking, but he was a strange boy. "Why?" she asked again.

"Why aren't they bonded?" he asked. "My father, Silverfox is his name, loves his queen, but she doesn't care for him. When they were together he bonded with her but she rejected him. Ravens do that. We deliberately mislead one another."

"Why?" Kara felt like a child pestering an adult about why the sky was blue and not purple but she wanted to know. Come morning, she wouldn't remember it, but that was then and this was now.

"Power," said Lucien. "Madea wanted Silverfox's loyalty... I'd rather not talk about it if it's all the same to you."

"I'm sorry, I just... never mind."

"Sorry."

"It's okay," Kara said. But she caressed his face and watched him close his eyes and felt him press into her hand.

She leaned forward and put her lips to his. Scarlet eyes flew open but he didn't pull away from her. His mouth was tight and wouldn't open but his heart fluttered.

"I can't," he breathed, yet still pressed against her.

When his mouth opened, ever so slightly, it was as if she'd taken a sip from a mountain stream dipped in honey—faintly sweet and so clean. But not cold though as she felt fire.

"I can't." He finally tore himself away from her. "Please don't do that." He wiped his mouth but closed his eyes and smelled his hand. "Fuck," he whispered. "I'm going to go for a walk." He got up.

"Lucien?"

"Kara, you don't want me. You want to be human and forget me. Please don't fuck with me. It's unkind." He gestured at the cottage. "Better go inside. It's cold outside." Then he walked away, disappearing into the night.

The kiss had rattled her. An odd sensation tightened between her legs. It made her want to squeeze her thighs together, shudder, and grind onto the wooden boards of the porch. That was silly, of course, and after the feeling subsided she got up and pulled the door to her new home.

The room upstairs was to be Kara's. A real bed with clean sheets, a vanity with an unbroken mirror in the corner, and a soft wool rug on the floor—it was wonderful. When she opened a blue wooden door, it was a bathroom with spotless white tiles on the floor. She'd live here... she thought she'd be happy. Maybe happiness was for those with hearts.

She washed her face and was putting away the single sequin dress she had in a closet and changing into a cotton one borrowed from Eilis when there was a knock at the door. She had a door. That made her smile at least.

She opened it and Lucien was in the hallway.

"Come on in," she said cheerfully.

He passed by her without a word and closed the door behind himself. He sat on her bed, then flicked his watch. "Well, come on." He scooted back on the bed, then tapped his thigh. "Lay your head here. I need to be touching your crown."

"Now?" Kara frowned, shooting a look back at the bath water she was running.

"I have to leave soon and I won't be back." He shrugged. "I have other shit to do."

"Oh."

Kara hesitated. Something akin to fear tied her feet to the wooden boards of the floor. What if he killed her? She shook her head. No, he wouldn't. The thought of not remembering anything was... scary. But that was better, wasn't it?

"Kara?"

"Yeah."

She went to the bathroom to close the water to the tub, looked at herself in the mirror above the basin, then made up her mind. The mirror had reminded her just how much she hated the faerie.

When she came out, Lucien was looking through her satchel. Her many hearts were spilled on the checkered green sheets. "I have to take this," he said. "Is there anything you *have* to keep?"

She understood what he was saying: she couldn't have keepsakes from her old life. Why would a human who had a heart collect *tchotchke* tokens? She shook her head.

"I'll leave your *dinne* and pipe here, all right?" He pulled the dark wooden drawer by the bed and set the items inside.

"Does it hurt?" asked Kara.

Lucien lifted his scarlet gaze. "I won't hurt you."

The hem of Eilis's long cotton dress brushed the floor as Kara crossed the room and sat down next to Lucien on the bed. She thought of kissing him one last time but the way he looked, cold and agitated, she knew he would turn away from her if she tried.

So instead, she laid her head down on his lap. It was a lot of trust for someone who had none. But he'd brought her this far. She got to fly in an airplane, saw a child laugh, and had dinner with free humans. *It's enough,* she decided. And closed her eyes.

He ran his hand through her hair. Then his warmth cupped the back of her head, holding her skull like a bowl in his hand. *"Let me in,"* she heard him inside her mind.

Memory

Kara had never known her mother's name because Whiteswoon called her 'slave', and her mother responded to it. She never spoke to Kara and moved about their oceanfront estate as a maid, straightening after Whiteswoon, his generals, and his lycans. The nameless woman had a cross tattooed on both of her forearms, and a scythe inked on her neck. With long, thick, coarse black hair and large brown eyes, her mother had brown skin as if the sun loved her. Despite her warrior appearance, a docile woman she'd been who washed Whiteswoon's feet in a bucket with a soft sponge and kissed his knee when he asked.

When she was little, Kara had thought that was what love was—respect. But as she grew older and learned about glamour, she became convinced that Whiteswoon had mind control over her mother.

"Isn't that wrong?" she'd asked Blackhunt, one of Whiteswoon's generals that she used to spar with.

"Define wrong," the faerie said, easily parrying Kara's wooden blade and catching her with a knee to the sternum. He was tall and she was thirteen. "Do you think you have lungs? Do you think you need to breathe? Is that why you're panting?" He kicked again, making her tumble on the ground.

"The faerie breathe." Kara got up and dusted herself off, readying her stance again.

"Yes, we do. But your father doesn't. Do you want to be weak like a slave or take after the king?" Impossibly fast, he whacked his wooden staff across her back. "Had that been a blade, I'd have cut you in half."

"Why sire me from a slave at all?" Kara's wooden blade clashed against Blackhunt's.

Kara, or Judecca as her father had named her, had expected the answer to be something along the lines of Whiteswoon experimenting with a new breed of faerie but Blackhunt had said, "That's how much he hates her."

On her fifteenth birthday, two lycans she had fancifully named Girl and Boy because they had no names, baked her a cake and clapped their paws when she blew out the candles. Kara had been trying to learn how to read. Although Whiteswoon had a library of human books, no one would teach her human letters, and sometimes she sat alone in the library for hours trying to decipher the book her father liked to read.

"*Inferno,*" she heard Lucien in her mind. "*That's the name of the book you're holding.*"

"*What is it about?*" Kara asked.

"*Hell.*"

Whiteswoon hoarded art. He'd enslaved some humans to paint his portraits but had flayed them when they drew him ugly. Pretending to be a creature of the Maker, he liked paintings of angels because they had wings like him and were beautiful like him. He also loved mirrors and the piano.

On her sixteenth birthday there was a solar eclipse. High noon turned to grey dusk, the light falling by the seconds as a black circle slid across the sun, and nocturnal animals started, momentarily confused.

Kara had been home, and the vibrant blue oceanfront view of the terrace turned dark as she stood on the balcony gripping the copper railings. Her mother had been cleaning and oiling Whiteswoon's armor in the living room behind her, but Kara heard her drop it, the titanium vibrating as it hit the hardwood floor.

The palm trees turned to black hands in the dusk and when Kara looked back, her mother was gone. Kara ran through the estate knowing there was something wrong and looking for her—she'd never leave her father's armor on the floor.

Whiteswoon had been in the basement. New humans had been captured and brought to him, a husband and a wife, and he'd been trying to train them when her mother poured gasoline into the basement and set it on fire. Being a dungeon it had bars, and she'd locked them. She burned the whole house down, the husband and wife too, and Boy and Girl turned to cinders, but not Whiteswoon. He'd burst out of the ashes of his home untouched even by the soot.

Her mother had run away but she didn't get far, and Blackhunt brought her back by the time Whiteswoon was done inventorying his surviving art. Kara had been with him, trying to dig a hole for Boy and Girl. She'd wanted him to know she wasn't a traitor.

Kara thought Whiteswoon might beat her mother, but she'd mostly hoped that he was going to glamour her, unharmed.

But she'd spat in his face, screaming, "Vamperish immortalis!"

He killed her. He ripped her skin off and then ate her heart. Kara had never known her name or why she'd said that.

"It's a salute to the Raven queen," she heard Lucien. *"And her name, your mother's name, was Gabriela Arriaga, the Fae Slayer. She founded*

the Resurgence when she was eighteen. She was thirty years old when she went missing on a mission. In twelve years, she accomplished more than most men do in a hundred lifetimes. Humanity survived because of her."

"How do you know this? She died years before you were born," Kara asked.

"I've seen photographs of her. She lives forever because she will never be forgotten."

Kara's twin blades, *Nar* and *Sar* had flown at her father then, but she was halfblood and he was not. He beat her, imprisoned her in an iron cage for seasons, sliced off every part of her which would grow back, and harmed her in a way that would never heal. He hated humans, loathed her mother, and had lashed out at her—for years.

The human woman who'd nursed Kara, Rosa, had been religious. She'd been a nun before she was a slave. Rosa, a lean woman who wore a black shawl over her hair, stole the key from Whiteswoon and helped Kara escape, but she was so terrified of the faerie king's wrath that she wanted to die rather than try running.

She'd begged Kara, shoving a little blade into her hand because Rosa's faith didn't allow her to take her own life. Kara had obliged by sliding the knife through Rosa's ribcage, into her heart, then ran from home. She flew over the Atlantic to get away from Whiteswoon.

Initially, she'd been looking for the Resurgence but found the Bloods instead. She'd never seen vampires before then and had been relieved to find they looked human, acted human, and used to be human for the most part. They were the Maker's children, but cruelty didn't escape them. She'd been in Lyon when the nest turned pale. She'd been in two other nests before Nocturne, but once in the city of the night, time had escaped from her.

And all that ugliness, she let Lucien see because he'd promised her, and she trusted him. He turned off her memories like lights in rooms, turning dark as they dissipated.

Gabriela Arriaga, Kara repeated to herself as if she could will herself to remember it.

Her eyes closed, Kara felt tears wet her temple. *"I never knew her name. Thank you."*

"If you see Whiteswoon, you will recall him," Lucien said. She wanted to argue but he wasn't speaking to her then. He was commanding her. *"If you see him or anyone from his court who would recognize you, you will remember yourself and them. It's so you have a fighting chance, Kara, don't resist me.*

"Otherwise, you are a nineteen-year-old human girl. Your pulse is weak because you have a heart condition. You are allergic to baker's yeast, so don't eat anything containing it. We've never met but if you see me, you'll dislike me."

"Lucien, why?"

"When you wake in the morning, you will smile because you are happy. These are my orders, and you will obey me."

Then all the rooms in Kara's mind turned pitch black and her nocturnal sight wasn't so good. She was falling through the darkness, falling and falling. She thought there had been someone in her room, placing her head on the pillow and blowing out the candles. She heard the curtain close, the door open and shut, but they were just noises. Then, letting go of the things she could no longer recall, Kara fell asleep and had a dream.

She dreamed of a boy with scarlet eyes and chestnut locks, his name fading as she grasped at it. His face turned dark, and then she dreamed about her parents who died at sea, and Uncle Sean who'd taken her in. From now on, she'd try her best to be good and help out around the stead. The Doyles were kind, and she didn't want to trouble them. That was ingrained in her, that she didn't want attention or trouble.

Keep

Lucien had seen worse. Arriaga and Whiteswoon hadn't been his parents, so there was some emotional distance. *It's not so bad,* he told himself as he drove to the Raven Keep. Leaving Kara had been difficult, and knowing she wouldn't recognize him when they met next, more so. Driving home was hard because he found himself alone, again. Hopeful thoughts such as introducing himself to Kara again swiveled in his mind, but he crushed them because he was no longer a child. *It's not so bad. It doesn't hurt.*

He crossed the wooden bridge over Boyne River, the imposing dark mass of the thousand-year-old castle, Raven Keep, falling on the surface beginning to shimmer from the silver light of dawn.

Guards on the turrets and soldiers manning ballistae with iron harpoons on the battlement shouted, and a spotlight shone into his car, blinding him momentarily before the heavy iron netting of the front gate lifted.

"Cutting it close aren't you, Lucien?" a man in a Resurgence green uniform asked as Lucien parked in the front drive and got out.

He had forgotten his name because he was one of the day guards and he rarely crossed paths with them. "Sorry," was all he said.

He rushed across the courtyard to bang on the tall iron door of the keep.

"You're late, boy," he heard Lasso say before the door clanked open. A slit only large enough for Lucien to slide through appeared before Lasso was locking up again, the gate bar grating across the metal hooks.

The castle of a human lord from the dark ages had been renovated extensively after the Ravens took over a century and a half ago, at the onset of the Bloodline War. Lucien had been born here and spent his entire life at the Raven Keep, but his home greeted him as a stranger.

Lasso, a large man in a long, black coat and equally dark braids sneered at him, his red eyes a menace in the candlelight of the stone hall. "Where are Andre and Dedreh?"

"Dead," said Lucien, eyeing Ade up on one of the high windows, squatted like a gargoyle statue. The windows in the hall had iron shutters and no longer opened or brought light, but the arches the humans built remained.

"What do you mean dead, boy?" Ade leaped down. Ade the Nightmare he was called, and the pureblood's crimson eyes burned like hot coals against his skin the color of the night. The twist of his lips bared long white fangs.

"I need to speak with the queen." Lucien tried to step around Ade, but he shoved him into the door.

"What do you mean, dead?" Ade yelled and his voice echoed, bouncing off the silent walls. Dedreh had been his friend.

Lucien moved Ade's hand that was clutching the front of his shirt and pushed him. "I said, I need to speak with the queen. Let me through."

Ade punched the door inches from Lucien's head but stepped aside with a long hiss. "When Madea steps down, Francis will silver you and I'd pay pretty *dinne* to watch it."

"Yeah, yeah, Vitali who bashed your friend Dedreh's head in with a silver bat shared your sentiment," Lucien said in passing and kept walking. Francis's men hating him wasn't a new thing.

Two stories up, Aoife, the queen's handmaiden and a fullblood with pleasant soft brown eyes apologized. "The queen is resting, I'm sorry." She smiled and gave a small bow. "Perhaps you should too, Lucien. It's daylight outside."

Lucien flicked a look at the carved oak door behind Aoife, closed as it always was. "How is she?" He kept his voice low.

"The queen is well," Aoife said, but she pursed her lips and shook her head. "You'd best go," she whispered.

Lucien started the motor so he could heat some water to soak in the bath and wash off the filth of the den. When he closed his eyes, three lycans and their faerie master stared back at him. He wished there was a way to clean his own mind, shed it off like dirty clothes. Then he lay in his room and fell asleep watching The Wizard of Emerald City and woke up when the TV went quiet. It wasn't his television. It was his power, and the room was pitch dark.

The door creaked open and Silverfox stepped in holding a lantern. When he set it on the floor and closed the door his shadow traveled across the wall as he approached Lucien's bed.

Grumbling from the residual aches from having his body broken by Vitali, then carved by the faerie, Lucien sat up and rubbed his face. He squinted at Silverfox, the gold raven brooch pinned onto the front of his long black cloak gleaming. Except for Silverfox's white curls to Lucien's brown, people said they looked alike. But Lucien didn't think so.

"Did you turn off my motor?" Lucien asked, looking for his slippers on the floor.

"Madea's sleeping. It's too loud," was all he said as he pulled a chair, dragging the legs on the wooden floor, and sat down across from Lucien, the shine on his immaculate leather boots almost glinting like a weapon when he crossed his legs. He adjusted the twin *reapers* hanging from his belt to sit more comfortably.

"She's always sleeping," Lucien mumbled. "It's a wonder how she's still alive with all the sedatives she takes."

"Shut your mouth about my queen," Silverfox warned. "What happened in Nocturne? You're about to be blamed for the deaths of Andre and Dedreh."

"I didn't silver them. Vitali did."

"But it's your duty to protect the men under your command, no?"

"I was drugged, Silverfox," confessed Lucien. "I'd say Francis conspired to have me silvered but it's more likely that Madea's authority has corroded that much. There was a faerie in Nocturne and the Bloods had allowed him in. I don't think they're answering the queen's call. But that's just me."

Silverfox considered this, slipping off his leather gloves and reaching into his cloak to produce a pipe. "Recount for me the events precisely as they occurred."

Lucien reported the events of Nocturne, leaving out Kara, and lying that the Blood was walked in the sun by the faerie they invited when things didn't go their way. Silverfox only protected Lucien because their fates were undeniably tied, but his loyalty would not extend to covering for him should he find out Lucien had brought a faerie halfblood home.

At the cusp of nightfall, Lucien was in Silverfox's study with shelves of books, wool carpet, and candles burning in birdcages—no birds, just cages for the dramatics. He had no chairs except the one he was sitting on because he liked to make people feel uncomfortable. Lucien stood by the mockup of the solar system, rotating the moon around the earth.

"Solar eclipse lasting three days," he said. "That's not possible."

"The faerie portal affects gravity," Silverfox said with a pipe in his hand. He was smoking almost as much as Madea these days, always exhaling a red mist of *krystallis*. "It will lock the moon in its rotation for the length."

"Says who?" Lucien frowned. "And how does everyone know this? Do you ever question that?"

"Madea has foreseen victory and so has Francis. Faerie magic wanes during the eclipse."

Recalling from Kara's memory how Whiteswoon's glamour had blinked during the eclipse, and lost control of Arriaga, Lucien could believe that. It was the length of the eclipse that was hard to swallow.

"What do you think of premonitions?" Lucien asked.

Silverfox knocked his tongue with a grimace. He didn't speak, but Lucien heard him in his mind. *"It's bullshit."*

Now that Silverfox had laid a bridge between their minds, Lucien could return the silent words in kind. *"You don't believe Francis about the victory at Groom Lake, do you?"*

"I believe he believes it."

"Silverfox..." Lucien pleaded but Silverfox broke the connection.

A soft knock came on the door, and Aoife stepped in to announce, "Queen wants you, Lucien."

Braziers burned along the walls lined with Raven elders, and Queen Madea was on her throne of jagged black crystals on the dais. Francis stood to her right, leisurely leaning an elbow on the crest of the throne. The only Raven to dress in all white, he had long, straight, blond hair to Madea's midnight black curls, the result of them having different fathers.

The queen's tall lace collar came up to her cheeks like fingers crawling up, and every inch of her skin was layered in black silk except for her discolored face. Sunlight healed poorly on vampires and half of her face was milk white and the other half earth toned. Although she strummed the armrest of her throne with long nailed fingers as if someone was home, her mind was blank. Her red gaze was glassed over, and Lucien wasn't sure that she recognized him as he strode the length of the throne room and took a single knee in front of the dais.

"Vamperish immortalis." He bowed his head and tapped his heart before rising.

Silverfox went to stand on the other side of the throne, and the fact he hadn't been called before Francis said much to the fifty somewhat purebloods lined along the walls, their hands clasped behind their backs.

"How do you answer for the deaths of Ravens directly under your command?" asked Francis.

Lucien swung his gaze at the queen, but she was inspecting the gold caps on her fingers, disinterested or just lost.

"I take full responsibility," said Lucien, not wanting Francis to dig at it. Kara was on his mind. Silverfox knew the Bloods were betraying the queen. He would inform her in private, and hopefully, she would comprehend.

"Elaborate, Lucien. What do you mean?" asked Silverfox, his blond brows knotting.

"Vitali killed them. The Bloods do not answer the queen's call," said Lucien. "But I should have foreseen it. The failure is mine."

Francis sniggered at that. "You can't foresee the hand that is about to slap your face, boy. You're the dullest and the most untalented Raven I'd ever seen in all my long years. I'm not surprised. In that regard, I say the fault is not yours but the one who sired you." He smirked at Silverfox. "Who sent you on such a delicate mission, so clearly far above your head, boy?"

It had been the queen who'd told Lucien that Vitali and Sedric were 'just boys' and asked him to fly there only taking two chaperones. But it was Francis's mission, everyone knew so. Yet, undermining Madea and Silverfox was the arrogant bastard's favorite pastime.

"Over your head, Francis. As far as I know, you're a simple attaché," said Lucien.

Francis put his hand on Madea's shoulder and she looked up at him and smiled. "This boy has caused the deaths of two Ravens. What should his punishment be?" Francis asked sweetly.

Madea frowned at Lucien, then said, "Silver him."

"Queen," Silverfox called from the other side. "He's pureblood. The deaths are of fullbloods."

"Pureblood?" asked Madea, tilting her head. She didn't recognize him. "He's young. Perhaps just flog him. But child, learn to take the lives of those you command seriously."

"I do, Queen." Lucien bowed.

"Apparently not," hissed Francis.

Sometimes elders grew wary of time and walked out into the sun, but Madea was only twenty years older than Francis. Whatever was wrong with her mind, she'd done it to herself, and sometimes Lucien resented her for it. She'd walked out into the sun willingly and her injuries were grievous. Perhaps her brain had fried as well but that happened well over a century ago and Lucien was only twenty-four. She had always been *this* for as long as he could recall. He didn't have a single memory of her being lucid.

"How many lashes?" Silverfox asked, to not leave it to Francis.

"A hundred." Madea said a random number, making it worse. A smile danced on Francis's thin lips.

"The standard for the most outrageous crime is fifty, Queen," advised Silverfox, disheartened.

"He's committed two outrageous crimes," argued Francis.

"I can still count, Silverfox," said the queen.

To Lucien's right, the grin on Ade's face widened. All eyes were on him. "My queen is fair, and I gladly accept her sentencing," said Lucien.

He was commanded to take off his shirt, which he did, and his hands were cuffed to a hitching post like a horse.

"Open wide," said Lasso, and stuffed a dirty rag into Lucien's mouth, making him gag.

Francis had a nine-tailed whip which Lucien had tasted before, but as it cracked through the air and snapped on his skin, he yelped. The tassels had hidden silver hooks and Lucien felt the burn as it grated across his skin.

It cracked again, and again. Lucien knew Francis well enough to know what this was: a setup. He wanted him to cry for Silverfox and start a confrontation. The queen wouldn't care and Silverfox with less than fifteen purebloods under his command to Francis's thirty-five would look weaker if he confronted Francis and had to back down. All of it was meant to undermine Madea and make her heir appear weak, so Lucien gritted through it as the silver hooks scraped his flesh and tore it in gashes.

'This will scar,' Kara had said. *'I didn't mean just your body.'*

He had many and now he would have a hundred more.

It's all right, he tried to convince himself as his mother sat indifferently on the throne, ironing out a wrinkle in her dress with her fingers. She didn't care. She never had.

Silverfox had turned to the side and lowered his gaze, wincing ever so slightly with each lash but not disobeying his queen. Kara was the only person, ever, to comfort Lucien when he was hurt. Perhaps it wasn't so pathetic that he missed her so much.

Thirty-seven, he counted, before darkness began enveloping his vision. He couldn't faint in front of everyone, but it hurt, and it hurt incredibly.

It's not so bad.

It doesn't hurt.

It's not that bad.

Lucien was in his room. He didn't remember how he got there but The Wizard of Emerald City was playing on his TV, the journey unfolding on the yellow brick road, when Aoife came to give him a glass of warm blood.

Thank you, he thought but didn't know if he'd actually said it. Aoife set the glass on the floor by his bed and left. Francis was cruel, that wasn't new. His mother didn't care and that wasn't new. But somehow it hurt worse for having known Kara. The girl had come back for him twice and she didn't know him from a hole in the wall. He wanted to be cared for, wanted to feel the way he did when she kissed him.

It's not that bad.

He drank the blood. It didn't help the pain any. So he smoked diamorphine till he was high enough to think Kara was in the room, sitting by the bed and stroking his face, and fell asleep with the TV on. But the film was over by then, the screen blank.

Slayer

Lucien drove through Summerset at night as the rain tapped on his windshield and Louis Armstrong sang in the car. He passed through the night strip bright with tavern signage, drunk men stumbling out, and women in bright clothes laughing, and pulled into a dark parking lot of a warehouse-like building. Flat roofed and uninspiring it was, but the windows were alight.

Resurgence operated with Ravens in mind which meant everything was open twenty-four hours. A woman in a green uniform greeted him when Lucien pushed the door open and a copper bell chimed. He went to the ticketing booth, but the woman who'd greeted him said, "It's free for Ravens."

"Are you the tour guide?" he asked.

"Yes." The woman smiled. She was in her thirties and wore a black beret on her ginger crown, the thick orange braid coming down to her chest. "How can I help you?"

"Will you show me around?" he asked and handed her a thousand *dinne* for her troubles.

She blushed but accepted. "I've never met a pureblood." She tucked imaginary hair behind her ear. "Welcome to the museum in honor of Gabriela Arriaga, the Fae Slayer, Mother of the Resurgence."

In soft yellow light, human weapons were displayed in glass casings, from the primitive rifles to the fae-tracking rocket launchers, and as the tour guide whose name was Jennifer explained the displays, pointing with her white gloved hand, Lucien's gaze settled on the grand poster on the wall. Gabriela Arriaga, larger than life, depicted with a gun in each hand, a tattoo of a cross on each arm, and one of a scythe on her neck.

There were many photographs of her on the wall, some Lucien had seen in the archives, but others new to him. A particular image of her and Madea drew his attention. The black and white photograph of a century ago had captured Madea laughing. With a white feather in her hair, his mother looked young, but she would have been nearly seven hundred years old at the time and Arriaga twenty-five. The queen was ancient now but why had she aged so much in a mere century?

"Tell me about Arriaga," said Lucien because Jennifer was explaining weapons and he knew all of it already.

"Reverent Mother Gabriela Arriaga was born in La Paz, Mexico. It's along the Gulf of California." She pointed at a dot in a red peninsula on a map. "Red marks faerie territory. The first appearance was in Groom Lake, a military base in the lost continent. Both the north and south Americas were lost in the first decade of the Bloodline War." She gestured over the map. "Then the Asias. We've lost contact with Africa and Australia. Some say it's a human haven free of faerie, but others say it's a tall tale. The Resurgence had flown many missions over the lost lands and found no signs of organized human settlements..."

Her words wavered, then she blushed. "I'm sorry. You must know all this. This is too basic?"

He did know all this. "Can you tell me more about Arriaga?"

"She was the first contact between the vampires and the humans. She negotiated for the Trinity and led the unified force against the faerie. Gabriela Arriaga found and burned Whiteswoon's nest here." She tapped on the map. "It is said that she killed over two hundred faeries that day, a grand victory for the Trinity."

"Killed fully grown faerie or burned their eggs?" asked Lucien. The faerie females didn't carry their young to term but deposited them into egg-like shells they built of human or animal remains, to eat as they grew.

"Does it matter?" Jennifer blinked. "The only good fae is a dead fae. The younger we get them, the better it is."

She killed Whiteswoon's children, Lucien thought. Then he shook his head to clear the sentiment. The faerie didn't have children. But for one, maybe.

"Right." Lucien smiled. "How did she die?"

"She lives," Jennifer insisted. "The Fae Slayer is immortal."

"Of course."

They ended up together at a tavern a block away. Red walls and black stools at the bar, and Jennifer slapped him on the back when she thought he was funny. It stung, and he winced. After a bottle, he bit her neck in the bathroom stall.

She invited him up when he drove her home, but he waved her goodnight. He'd never been with anyone because he didn't want to bond. He didn't want to end up as Silverfox, crawling on hands and knees for someone who didn't love him back. Despite having bedded Silverfox and conceived Lucien, Madea didn't have a single care for either of them. Because had she loved, she wouldn't be so fucked all the time. Because had she cared, Francis wouldn't have flogged Lucien with a silver tipped whip. It hadn't been the first time he'd been at the receiving end of Francis, and it wouldn't be the last either.

Drunk and beside himself, Lucien drove to Sean's cottage by the cliff. He parked his car in the woods and walked to the white stone cottage, pale in the thick of night. He shouldn't have done that, but he did anyway.

Seeing all their windows were dark, Lucien didn't want to disturb the Doyles and had been sitting on the autumn grass, wilted but wet from the rain that had just passed over, when he heard footsteps behind and turned.

It was Kara in a denim overall and flat-heeled shoes. Her bleached blonde hair was in pigtails. "Hey," she said, approaching him despite having been ordered to dislike him on sight. "Are you all right?"

"Is Sean home?" he managed, getting up and unsuccessfully wiping the grass stains from his pants and smudging the wet dirt.

"No, Uncle is staying over at work and Riona and Auntie are with him," she said. "Who are you?"

"Why are you up so late?" Lucien asked but his question answered itself when a drunk farm boy stumbled out of the woods, fiddling with his belt.

"Should I tell Uncle a Raven was looking for him?" Kara asked.

"No, it's okay." Lucien headed to his car. He was stupid for having come here.

"Do you want to come in?" Kara asked. "Dawn is awfully close."

"Hey, Kara." The drunk boy draped his heavy arm around her shoulders. "Why not invite me in?"

"Because you can walk home in the light," she said. "And I've told you not to piss on my aunt's bale."

The drunk boy grabbed Kara's arm and Lucien hissed, baring his fangs in anger, but Kara clocked the boy square in the jaw, and the boy as heavy as cattle fell on his ass.

"Go home, Jonah, you're drunk," she said.

Mumbling, cursing, he crawled away, mostly because Lucien was there, and staggered out of sight in the moonlight.

"I didn't get your name." Kara turned to Lucien. "But you'd better come on in. The songbirds are starting."

"Why don't you obey me?" He frowned. "You're supposed to dislike me."

Kara didn't hear him and opened the door to the cottage, turning to say, "Come on, Pureblood, I won't bite you, but I bet you the sun will."

Lucien had meant to say 'no' and walk back to his car. He didn't have time to drive back to the Keep, but he could have found shelter at any other building in Summerset. But it was impossible to walk away with Kara keeping the door open and waiting for him. He wanted her to touch him again, glide her fingers on his skin, and act as if she cared. There was no harm so as long as he wasn't intimate with her, he convinced himself, and followed Kara in.

As Lucien settled on the daybed with a flowery futon in the living room, he heard Kara walk around the house putting the wooden storm shutters on the windows. The Doyles had a simple living space with white plastered walls and light furniture huddled around the fireplace. Kara came in, tossed her shoes by the door, lit an oil lamp, and set it on the dark wooden table. She'd adjusted well, behaving as if she'd lived here a long time.

"Is Sean treating you well?" Lucien asked.

Kara wiped the table, fetched him a glass of water, then sat down next to him. "What's your name?"

"Lucien."

"Drink water, Lucien. You're drunk."

Lucien took a sip and cleared his throat, then sat with the glass of water in his hand, awkwardly. "So... was that your friend back there?"

"Jonah?" asked Kara, taking the ribbons out of her hair and massaging her scalp. "Yeah, he's the neighbor's boy. 'Haven't met anyone from Browndowry', he says. He took me to the fair. Boys are just curious because I'm new here."

"You're from Browndowry?"

"Uncle says." Kara shrugged. "I have a problem with my mind sometimes." She knocked on her head. "Had a boating accident when I was a girl. Also, my heart hurts all the time."

"Your heart hurts?" Lucien frowned. Inadvertently, he reached and felt for a pulse on her neck—she had none.

"No, silly. Here." She took his hand and placed it over her chest.

Even if she didn't have a heartbeat he could feel her breathing, her skin warm underneath the thin cotton shirt. They held each other's gaze, then she leaned slowly toward him, and he closed his eyes. Whatever control he had faltered. If he could just have her... it wouldn't be so bad to crawl for eternity.

"Do you have any *krystallis*?"

He opened his eyes, and she was just looking at him. The way a girl would look at her uncle's coworker. Nothing like the way she looked at him on the porch when she kissed him. This was his fault. He was stupid.

"Yeah." He dug through his coat pocket, took out a bag, and put it on her palm. "I'm going to go." He got up.

"Suit yourself," she said, suddenly not caring about the light outside. She'd just wanted *krystallis*. She saw a vampire and thought he might have a fix. She was right, of course.

"Bye, Kara."

"Yeah." She was looking down and loading her pipe.

Lucien walked out into the dawn and closed the door. He sat in his car and started it but didn't go anywhere. Leaning over the steering wheel, he watched the horizon brighten over the deep blue ocean, loud and thundering against the steep cliffs.

The sound of another car approaching, Sean, made Lucien drive off. Riona was ten years old, and he'd known her since she was born. There was no need for the little girl to see him burning in her driveway.

Some miles away, Lucien pulled over to the side of the dirt road and crawled into the trunk of his car. In the small dark space, he folded and hugged his knees. Then, he cried.

Father

"Lucien, where are you?"

He heard Silverfox and opened his eyes. He was still in the trunk. Not that he could see in pitch black, but he could feel the space. Silverfox's range was a couple of miles, maybe, so he was in Summerset.

"Where are you?" Lucien asked.

"I'm at the Doyles's. I thought you might have come here. His niece says you were drunk and left at dawn."

Fuck. Kara. Lucien opened the trunk and then winced—he hadn't checked for light. Only after he was getting into the driver's seat and slamming the door did it occur to him that if Silverfox was out and about it would be night, but he hadn't thought of that when he first opened the trunk. He could have gotten blasted with daylight and that was stupid.

"I'm on my way."

He was only a few miles from the Doyles's cottage, but the drive felt longer for his heart raced the entire time. Silverfox was keen, as sharp as they came, and he didn't want him anywhere near Kara, or even Sean for that matter.

As he pulled up to the brown patch of earth that was the driveway, Kara was trying to ride a bicycle and failing while Riona pointed at and laughed at her.

"I used to know how to ride, I swear!" Kara yelled, veering off into some shrubs.

An unknown male, a Resurgence fighter from the haircut, pulled Kara up from the shrubs and straightened the bicycle for her. They were laughing. She was beautiful, new, and looked to be drawing the whole neighborhood onto Sean's yard. There were three other men, all soldiers, probably buddies with the one bending to blow Kara's elbow that she'd scabbed.

"Hi, Lucien." She waved.

He ignored her and strode straight for the porch where Sean was sitting on the steps with a beer in his hand and Silverfox stood with his black-gloved hands clasped at his back. His black sedan with a gold raven on the hood was in the driveway with Poppy behind the wheel. The pureblood with a small face and deep, large doe eyes sneered when Lucien passed her by. She had long auburn hair, and Lucien imagined she might have been pretty had her eyes not been so large and so red. But Silverfox seemed to like her enough—she was his mistress. She would never bond with him so long as the queen lived but that was on her.

"What are you doing?" Lucien asked Silverfox. He didn't typically leave Madea's side and she *never* left the Keep.

"Getting some much needed fresh air," Silverfox said, turning to him. He exchanged some pleasantries with Sean, then guided Lucien to his car with a grip around his elbow.

"I'll just follow you," said Lucien.

"Leave your keys with Sean. He'll bring your Jag back to the Keep."

"Sure thing." Sean got up and caught Lucien's keys when he tossed them to him.

Seeing Kara accept beer from the soldier, Lucien said, "Alcohol is brewed with yeast, Kara. Don't drink anything unfiltered or undistilled." Whiskey and whatever Nebula had been were fine, but not unfiltered beer.

Kara mumbled something and returned the beer to the soldier, but that had caught Silverfox's attention and his eyes narrowed. Lucien was a step behind today. He ignored Silverfox and got in the car.

Poppy adjusted the rearview mirror so that Lucien and she were looking at each other in the reflection when she said, "You're a spoiled brat."

Her attitude shifted and she started the car when Silverfox got into the back seat next to Lucien. She hated Madea and, by extension, Lucien. In that regard, he didn't fault her for it. Madea wasn't fair. Not to Silverfox, not to anyone.

"Keep?" asked Poppy, leaving the Doyles's cottage behind.

"Thank you, Poppy," Silverfox answered.

Lucien felt nauseous and rolled down the window. He didn't get car sick. It was the hangover setting in.

"What are you doing out here, anyway?" Lucien asked.

Silverfox tossed a thing onto Lucien's lap. Picking it up, he saw it was a tassel from a whip with a little silver hook concealed inside.

"Why didn't you tell me?" asked Silverfox.

Lucien threw the tassel out of the window. "That's what he wanted. For me to cry and for you to interfere. He was trying to undermine you, as he always is."

"Yet you keep giving him cause enough to sink his fangs into," was what he said, but Lucien also heard, *I'll deal with him soon enough.*

Madea won't let you, Lucien thought. And when Silverfox didn't answer, Lucien stole a look, but he was turned away, staring out at the dark terrain passing by the window. "Silverfox?"

"I heard you," he hissed. Silverfox was angry... seething, matter of fact.

"Father?"

"It's fine," he snapped. "Close the window." He pulled out his pipe when Lucien obliged.

"Silverfox?" Poppy flicked a gaze in the rearview mirror.

"Yes?"

"Do you want me to stop by Devon's and get the whiskey you wanted?" They were passing through downtown Summerset.

"That would be wonderful. Thank you, Poppy. Lucien could use a drink as well, right?"

"No, thank you." He could have barfed at the thought of any liquor.

Poppy pulled in front of Devon's brewery, and after she left the car, Silverfox said, "You brought that girl with you. Tell me why?"

"What?" Lucien's heart nearly came out through his throat.

"People saw you and Sean pushing a crate around. You didn't bring it with you to the Keep and Sean didn't log the contents. Francis is sniffing your trail. Next time don't be so sloppy."

"She's just some girl I found wandering around alone on the mainland. I wanted to help her."

"That's fine. Just be more careful next time. Despite being called Raven Keep, you live in a den of wolves."

"Yeah," said Lucien and didn't he know it.

"Her mind is altered." Silverfox carried his gaze slowly and parked it on Lucien. "She believes she's Sean's niece and she's from Brown-dowry. The *weave* is impeccable, just enough seeds implanted for her mind to fancy the rest. It's more believable that way, truly intricate work." He smirked then patted Lucien's head.

"Not good enough, apparently," mumbled Lucien. It was frightening how astute Silverfox really was.

"Oh, it's not her. It's Sean and his wife. The young girl Riona doesn't know any different, but Sean and Eilis know they don't have a niece from Browndowry. I fixed them for you. You shouldn't leave witnesses."

"You can *weave* without physical touch?" Lucien's jaw dropped.

"We all have our talents, Lucien. Madea and Francis with their foresight, you as well. Mine is *weaving* memory. But the way you worked the girl, I believe you will be better than me with time." This was the warmest Silverfox had ever been with him.

Perhaps what Lucien needed all along to get his father's sympathy was a public flogging where he nearly died. Perhaps it was something else because Silverfox didn't look so miserable just then, cracking the window open to exhale a prolonged red mist and letting go of something else as well.

He's decided on something, Lucien thought privately. He knew Silverfox at least that much.

Not in the throne hall because Madea wasn't present, but in Francis's audience room where the candelabras on the wall reflected on the polished wooden floor like mirrors, Francis and General Mathis argued, the general aggressively pointing, spittle flying while Francis only sneered, occasionally checking his nails—he liked painting them black.

Lucien stood at the edge of the room with his back against the wall, as did the other Ravens, as did the general's men. It was a large space dressed in green velvet with gold crested furniture, and Francis lounged on a large divan, checking himself in the thorn framed mirror above the mantle of an unlit fireplace. Silverfox's back was to Lucien, but when he checked his reflection in the mirror he was frowning.

Daylight outside, Madea was asleep. General Mathis always came during daylight. A little show of authority, Lucien thought, to remind the Ravens that they needed the daywalkers. Lucien diverted his gaze when he saw Ade snarling at him from across the room.

"Ten hours of flight," the general said after he took a long inhale to calm himself. "Four." He showed the corresponding number of fingers as if explaining to a child. "Four freighters, and three cargo jets. With the sheer tonnage we need to haul across the Atlantic to support this operation of yours, we do not have enough fuel to return, and I will not commit the Resurgence to a one-way trip. Nah, no way.

"You say we can find fuel on that faerie wasteland. Maybe we can, maybe we can't, but that is not how I roll."

"Your men must be heavy. How much do you weigh, General?" asked Francis.

Mathis took a sharp inhale. "I need to carry vehicles, you twat. It's ninety miles to Groom Lake from the nearest landing sight. If you say you can kill Whiteswoon during the eclipse, let's pretend I believe you. But we can't get there, is what I'm saying."

"Then fly *to* the site, General, and do an airdrop," said Francis.

"*Do* an airdrop he says." The General turned to Silverfox. "This clown doesn't understand choppers can't cross the Atlantic without aerial refueling. Madea understands logistics. I need her word that this will work and that I'm not sending my men to die on a fool's errand. I need *her* to say that she'll bring back Whiteswoon's head for the amount of blood we're about to spill. Otherwise, it's a no go."

"I will personally inform the queen." Silverfox gave a small bow.

"Man to man, Silverfox, I hear rumors that her mind is unraveling and she's rarely seen lucid anymore. Is that true?"

"Of course not."

"Would you tell me if it was true?"

"Probably not." Silverfox smiled, and the general chuckled after a pause.

General Mathis, a man in his fifties, deep-voiced and tall but a child compared to Silverfox, put his hand on the Raven elder's shoulder and squeezed. "This is our third attempt at Groom Lake. The first two were spectacular failures. We used to be able to afford to throw a hundred and twenty thousand soldiers into an assault in the olden days. But no longer. We fail this, Resurgence is done, your covenant too.

"So make me believe in miracles, Silverfox. Because so far, I ain't buying what this twat is selling. Understood?"

"Your concerns will be addressed, General Mathis."

Mathis and Silverfox exchanged nods because Silverfox didn't shake hands, and turning his back to Francis, Mathis strode out, his men after him.

"Wake Madea," hissed Francis after the general was shown out of the keep.

"The day I begin taking orders from you, I'll be sure to let you know," said Silverfox, and infuriating Francis further, he turned his back and walked out.

His Ravens followed out, Lucien among them.

But then they held a closed meeting in Silverfox's library of cages, and Lucien was asked to step out. He went to his room and burned Kara's satchel and the hearts her 'friend' Star called tchotchke. One was porcelain and said, 'Be Happy'. She'd given it to him, and he wanted to keep it. Besides, it wouldn't burn anyway.

He snuffed the candles out and lay down in his bed holding the little thing. He sniffed it to see if it smelled like her. It did not. It smelled like the leather of the bag.

He tried to sleep but wanted to cry. So he got up and headed to the library to find Dante's *Inferno*. He knew of it but had never read it, and wanted to see why Whiteswoon would like it.

Dream

It's a ring in hell, Lucien realized. Whiteswoon had named his daughter Judecca after the innermost circle of hell. Arriaga's punishment, no doubt, but he had trouble grasping the mindset of a creature that would sire a child as a form of torment.

Sitting behind the oak table in the kitchen, the limestone tiles cool under his bare feet, he'd been reading *Inferno* alone in the candlelight while sipping blood. The kitchen, pots and pans hanging on a rack over the hearth, was used to cook for human guards and was quiet most of the time. Ravens, fullblood or pureblood, never came here. Because of the need for ventilation, the kitchen had one of the rare windows at the Keep that opened and a door that stepped out into the courtyard. But it was daylight outside and both were closed with wooden blinds. The frailty of the room was yet another reason that Ravens didn't frequent it.

He'd been contemplating Kara's name and what that said about the fae king they were meant to face at Groom Lake when he heard footsteps down the hall. Assuming it was one of the staff, he kept his face buried in the pages. He ignored it when the door opened.

"I never knew you liked to read."

He lifted his gaze. Madea in her white nightgown was by the door. She entered, leaving it open behind her.

"Queen." Lucien got up.

She motioned him down. He obliged.

"Do you want me to call Aoife for you, Queen?" Aoife was her caretaker.

Madea smiled. "No, just sit. I have a surprise, love."

"Yes, Queen."

"You know, you'd be a lot happier if you'd just accept her."

The thing had been sudden and he didn't know how to respond. Did she mean Kara? But how would she know?

"I see," Madea said. "How do I look?" She'd appeared incredibly lucid, but she turned to the wall and fixed a phantom crown on her head. There was no mirror there. Then she fidgeted with an imaginary train, but she was in her nightgown.

"Queen..." Lucien rose.

"I said it was fine, Silverfox. Stop making yourself a nuisance. I've foreseen her arrival. I told you she lived. You just hate being wrong, don't you?"

"I'm sorry," said Lucien, carefully backing away. He had to go find someone more qualified to deal with her, like Silverfox.

When he was quietly trying to pass by her, Madea grabbed his arm, looked straight into his eyes, and said, "I don't love you."

"Okay."

She was clawing into him but he didn't want to yank his arm from the queen and remained with her. Then she caressed his face and tried to kiss him. That time, he did pull away from her.

"Fine, be like that. You were always jealous of Gabe and wanted her dead, didn't you? Francis too. You're petty, Silverfox."

"I'm sorry." Lucien eyed the door. Why was the queen wandering around alone and where was Aoife?

Madea gasped, her eyes large. Her entire face brightened with happiness he'd never seen on her. "Do you hear that?" she asked, turning away from Lucien.

Right at that moment, both Silverfox and Francis rushed in through the door but before Lucien could take a breath of relief, Silverfox grabbed him and slammed him to the wall.

"There she is," he heard the queen say. He couldn't see her but saw Francis and the bewilderment on his face.

Sunlight flooded the room.

The dark silhouette of the woman he never knew stepped out through the door, out into the courtyard in high noon.

"Mom!" Lucien screamed, fighting Silverfox.

But he was stronger and held him pinned against the dark corner of the kitchen. "Let her go."

"Mom!" Lucien clocked Silverfox, twisting away and throwing him onto the floor. He ran for the door.

The queen was a candlewick in the courtyard, burning, motionless, and silent. Silverfox wrestled Lucien to the floor as the Ravens rushed in to close the door. He held him down as he wailed and screamed. "Mom!"

"Let her go, Lucien. She's gone," Silverfox kept saying. Then his knee was on Lucien's neck. "Calm down." Holding him down, Silverfox was suffocating him as well.

Snarling like a feral dog, Lucien grappled with Silverfox, tearing a chunk out of his arm at some point. But when he drew his *reaper,* the Raven elder had it with him, breaking Lucien's arm and knocking him out.

As Lucien fell through the darkness, he grasped at the memories of his mother, flailing as if someone was trying to take them from him. But no one was in his mind other than himself. He plummeted through the despair, alone.

Why, Mom? Why!

Before the sun set, before anyone went out to collect the queen's ashes from the courtyard, a fight broke out in the keep. Silverfox, who moved faster than a flying arrow, a blur of flurries with the trailing glint of the *reaper,* had the silver edge on Francis's throat.

Ade had Lucien's hair in his grip, his *reaper* pressed against Lucien's back. "Let him go!" Ade was yelling.

"You let my boy go!" Silverfox hissed.

The Ravens were at each other's throats, but Francis outnumbered Silverfox three to one. Lasso had an arrow nocked at Silverfox and Poppy had her *reaper* on Lasso's nape.

"Let's all bring it down a notch," Francis said, casually pushing Silverfox's *reaper* away. "You're outnumbered, Silverfox."

"I can still take you with me," said Silverfox. They were staring at each other.

"I agree," said Francis. "I don't want to fight you. I don't want to be short of Ravens when I go to Groom Lake. Tell me what you want, Brother."

"I'm not your brother," said Silverfox. "At nightfall, I walk out of here with my men and Lucien. You can have the throne. We do not contest your claim."

"You do not contest it *yet*," countered Francis. "I'd ask for your word, but I don't trust you to not silver me in my sleep. At nightfall, you and your men may leave. But Lucien stays..." He smirked. "To ensure your loyalty, Brother. After I return with Whiteswoon's head, after I'm voted king, you will have Lucien back alive, my word. In the meantime, bring Resurgence to me."

"With Madea gone, I can't promise it," said Silverfox.

"Try your best, Brother."

"Stand down, Father. I'm fine," Lucien said as Ade's *reaper* broke his skin and he felt the burn. "It's fine."

Lucien wanted Silverfox to leave, and maybe have a life with Poppy now that he was free of Madea. *Be Happy.* He thought of the heart in his drawer as his heart broke at the death of his mother. It didn't matter that she didn't love him. He loved her.

"I will speak to Mathis, but I cannot promise the Resurgence," said Silverfox and withdrew his *reaper.* "But I can promise your death should you harm Lucien. Have your throne, have a ball, but harm my boy and I *will* silver you."

"I believe you." Francis smiled.

Fiadh, Francis's blonde mistress, gloated as Francis sat down on the black throne and crossed his legs with an ankle over his knee—Madea hadn't been dead a day. Lucien wanted to collect her ashes and place them in an urn but was denied access to the courtyard. She'd lived nearly a thousand years but had left so little mark. Men's minds were fickle and so were their hearts. Everyone who was supposed to love and protect her judged her only by the bad years when her mind had been slipping. They acted as if they'd lugged off a giant burden, but a hole was punched through Lucien's heart.

Silverfox left at nightfall, but Lucien wasn't allowed to see him. Everyone knew each other's ability in Raven Keep and Francis's men were sure to escort Silverfox beyond the range he could communicate with Lucien.

In Francis's hall of green velvet divan with gold crest, the dark mirror over the mantle of the unlit fireplace, Ade pressed on Lucien's shoulder to make him kneel and sit on his heels while Francis lounged high up. Faidh, filling his empty cup, stood by him smugly.

"Tomorrow, right before high noon, there will be a solar eclipse and it will last for three days," Francis said. "Do you know how far out I saw that? Seven years, boy."

"Yet you didn't see Madea? You were right there. You came because you knew what she would do, and you let her burn anyway." Lucien's tears burned hot with hate. Ade struck him from the back but he didn't give a shit.

"How dare you?" Rage was in his voice but a smile danced across his lips, he couldn't help it. "Do you know what else I've seen? Victory. I kill Whiteswoon. He has long white hair and I see it wrapped around my wrist. I behead him." Francis acted out his fancy and Lucien said nothing.

"I'm going to save the world, Lucien." Francis checked his reflection in the glass he was holding. "And they'll paint me instead of the gods, generals, and kings. Resurgence, Silverfox, the Bloods, all will kneel in front of me and kiss my hand." He twirled his hand with the Raven ring. "A second Renaissance is coming to mankind, and I will lead it."

"You have delusions of grandeur, Uncle," said Lucien, and Ade burned him with silver.

"What does an ant understand of the intentions of men?" Francis cocked his head. "In the meantime, I don't need an enemy at my back. You will keep Silverfox in check for me."

"I don't matter to him. Ravens don't have parents."

"You matter to him because you're Madea's child," said Francis. "He loved my sister and that much is true." He clicked his tongue and nodded his chin at Ade.

Lucien was pulled up to his feet, his arms restrained by two Ravens he couldn't see as they'd put a bag over his head. He chose not to struggle. There was no point. It wasn't that bad anyway.

"Should your father betray me, you will know," he heard Francis, his voice distant as Lucien was hauled away.

After an hour-long drive where Lucien smelled the rain and the wet earth but saw nothing with a bag over his head, they put him in an iron coffin, latched the lid from outside, and buried him. Lifting his bound hands, he slipped the bag off his head but saw nothing in the pitch dark, only the sound of the earth being shoveled on top of him. He ran his fingers through the rough interior of the metal box he was in.

"Silverfox?" he called but Lasso answered instead. He didn't hear Lucien call. He'd just happened to speak.

"If you're not dug up tomorrow, you'll know Silverfox didn't cooperate. I hope he doesn't, and I hope you lie here for a hundred years and lose your mind in confinement. If we die, no one knows where you are."

"Why do you hate me? I hardly know you," Lucien asked.

"I loathe Madea. She bonded with a human over Francis, even over Silverfox. No one says it but everyone knows it. She was weak. It's well deserved that she walked out into the sun," he said then answered no more.

It was just Lucien alone in the dark. He had some oxygen canisters with him, but they'd run out at some point, he supposed, and then he would suffocate. His heart broke for Madea but when he finally fell asleep in the silence of it all, he dreamed about Kara.

Eclipse

Kara jumped on her pink bicycle with a white basket and silver tassels. It hadn't been given to her this way, but she'd decorated and made it hers.

"Don't be late!" Auntie called from the porch.

"Cotton candy in a bag!" Riona yelled. "Bubble gum flavor! Don't forget!"

Kara didn't want to be an apprentice to the artisan cheese maker. Rather, she wanted to join the Resurgence. She would start with Uncle Sean next week and he was going to enroll her in the aviation school, but in the meantime, everything was closing, expecting the three-day solar eclipse. The whole thing seemed spectacular. A lot of folks were gathering downtown to watch the event together and Kara was on her way to the market to meet with Declan, eat corndogs, have a fizzy drink, and go down to the ravine and smoke *krystallis*. Ravens had *krystallis*, and Resurgence worked with Ravens—not the whole reason she wanted to join the fight but that certainly helped.

With the wind in her face and sunshine above her head, Kara zoomed along the road, weaving through the horse-pulled carts and wagons.

They were also headed to the town. She wore Sean's green hoodie over her sundress because it was autumn, but the white skirt with yellow flowers flapped behind her like a nuisance flag, and she smiled. Her heart hurt. It always hurt, but if she moved fast enough, smiled bright enough, laughed loud enough, was obnoxious, hung out with boys, drank whiskey, and smoked diamorphine, it was sometimes better. She didn't tell Uncle Sean, otherwise he wouldn't let her go to aviation school.

But when she couldn't breathe from a sudden bout of sadness that wrapped around her chest like a cuirass a few sizes too tight, she pulled over and cried to make it better—a bit better. Then she pedaled to the market.

Meet me in St. Louis, she thought but that wasn't the name of the market. The market was just the 'Market', and the fair, the 'Fair'. But the bars, of which there were many, had names. Summerset had one of each thing and they were called by what they were. Auntie was a nurse at the 'Hospital'.

The market was busy, and Kara paid two *dinne* for a bag of bubble gum pink cotton candy and put it in the basket of her bicycle, closing and locking the lid. She didn't want to get high, forget, and disappoint Riona.

Underneath the auburn parasol of autumn trees rustling in the breeze, and the leaves glittering against the sun, Declan was sitting at the table with his friends, Patrick and Fin—they were all Resurgence. It was an outdoor tavern with wooden benches and long tables on the forest floor. Coal burned in iron braziers intermittently. The place was packed with all sixty somewhat tables fully occupied by the brightly dressed townfolk. Resurgence always had a table in any tavern and discount on all their drinks, as Kara had learned, and Declan waved from the best table in the spot, the one closest to the bar, a shed open on all four sides. Although it was afternoon, the yellow lights strung from trees were lit already, expecting the Longdark to begin soon.

Declan had a tan line on his ring finger but today he had a ring as well. When Kara flicked a look at it, he slipped it off and pocketed it. He was from Browndowry and Uncle Sean didn't know him well. He'd frowned at the tan line and told Kara not to see Declan anymore. But Uncle wasn't here, and Declan was fun.

"Hey, girl," he greeted her, draping an arm around her as she sat down next to him. He ordered her a beer and she had to remedy it, swapping it with a fizzy drink.

"Are you underage or what?" Patrick asked.

"No, I'm nineteen." Kara wiped the table where the glass had sweated.

"Your uncle's a nutbuster," said Fin.

"All pilots are assholes," said Patrick and they bumped fists.

"I'm going to be a pilot," said Kara, then thanked the waitress who brought her drink. "I'm sorry. Do you have any coasters?"

"It's an outdoor place, sweetie." She shrugged.

"Like to fly *high*?" Declan winked.

Kara smiled and let him kiss her neck.

"Yo, Sinclair!" Declan hollered. Throwing up his arm at a man passing by some tables away, he waved him over. "My buddy over here is a Redhawk," he bragged to Kara.

"I don't know what that means," Kara said.

"Means he's elite," Patrick clarified.

"Why are you still here, man?" Fin asked. "I thought you boys would be on your way off the continent."

Sinclair the Redhawk looked Resurgence from the haircut as he came over to the table, shaking his head. "What's up," he greeted the boys, then grimaced. "No one knows what's going on but Mathis issued a stand down. So, I guess we're not going." He shrugged with one shoulder. "Too bad though. I would have liked to waste some fae."

"Are the Ravens still going, or no one is going?" asked Declan.

"Don't know, man."

"What a waste of a perfect opportunity." Patrick spat.

The boys continued their chatter as Kara clutched her chest and exhaled slowly.

"Are you all right, or what?" Fin reached over to check her pulse.

Kara slapped his hand. "It's fine. I just have a heart condition. But don't touch me."

"Whatever," Fin mumbled. Then gulped beer.

"Mathis a pussy or what?" one of the boys said as Kara closed her eyes for a moment.

"Say that to the old man's face, man." Laughter followed.

Declan's arm fell away from her. The laughter stopped. Patrick had been saying something but trailed off midsentence. Everything went dead.

Kara opened her eyes and saw a shadow wipe across the table. She tilted her head back and saw everyone's face lifted to the sky. A black circle slid over the sun, turning it to a rim of faint glow, and the lights strung from the trees and the fire burning in the braziers brightened as midday gave way to late dusk in a single breath. Even the animals were silent.

Then a wolf or a dog howled in the distance and the night insects started.

"Wow," breathed one.

"Spectacular," said another.

A moment where the town held its collective breath passed and gave way to hooting, clapping, loud chatter, and everyone speaking at once.

The darkness stayed, and Declan proclaimed the eclipse would last three full days, but that wasn't what that was.

"That's not the moon's shadow," Kara thought out loud. "It's shadow art."

"Shadow art?" She heard Declan and he was frowning when she tore her gaze from the sky and settled it on his face. "Like fae magic shit?" he asked.

"Yeah, like fae magic shit," she whispered.

Fin knocked on the wooden table three times. "Don't say bad omen shit. It's just an eclipse. It happens."

"Not for three days," Kara insisted. She didn't even know what she was talking about. "It's shadow art." She was sure of it, but when she tried to recall how she would know it or who could pull such a *grand* feat of magic, her mind drew blank. An image of a white swan flapping its wings, but nothing else. She shook her head. Perhaps it was just one of the odd thoughts she sometimes had.

She tried to let it go and join the celebratory mood. Her heart had stopped hurting, which was good, but now her back bothered her. Her tattoo was itching, and she could *feel* the feathers stir under her skin. Then the blades on her arms pounded like a blacksmith's anvil. It was hurting inside her bones. She scratched at it till it turned red, but Declan caught her hand, smiled then kissed the skin she'd irritated.

"You're going to ruin your ink doing that. Do you want some lotion or something?"

"Those are badass," the waitress remarked, setting a glass of whiskey on the table.

"Badass ink for a top-notch girl." Declan's hand slid under her skirt. "Do you want to get out of here?"

"Yeah," said Kara, downing her drink. She was anxious and didn't want to be in a crowded place. "You said there was a ravine?"

"There sure is." He got up and tossed a few *dinne* on the table. "Do you mind if my friends join us?"

Kara was going to say, *'Two hundred and fifty, each,'* one of the more random things she said, but Fin grabbed Declan by the nape and whispered in his ear. Kara didn't hear him over the chatter but saw his lips, and he said, "Don't fuck with it. Her uncle is trouble."

"Who the fuck cares, I'm out of here in a week," Declan said.

"Let's go," she said and got up. Declan had promised her *krystallis* and she wanted it. She still had some left, tucked under her mattress, from when the Raven pureblood tossed it at her, but that was for rainy days, and it rained every day in her heart.

The stream, the moss on the rocks, and even the elms were all black in the Longdark. A mist began crawling on the forest floor. Declan breathed hot and heavy over her, beer and shellfish on his breath.

"Wait, wait." Kara twisted away when he tried to kiss her. "My *krystallis*?"

"I have it. I have it."

He hiked up her dress. She wasn't wearing anything under it.

"*Krystallis*, Declan."

"Yeah, yeah," he said, but he wasn't producing anything.

Kara didn't play like that. She twisted his arm and threw him off her, sending him cursing and tumbling. She got up and fixed her dress. She was just going to leave, but he charged out from the dark and punched her straight in the face—that surprised them both. She didn't even see him and was surprised.

"What are you?" He stared at her, stunned wide-eyed.

"What do you mean?"

"I'm a bare-knuckle boxing champion in my division."

"I don't know what that means. Do you have any *krystallis* or what?" When she held out her hand, he took a step back.

"No, I'm sorry." He looked frightened.

"I'm going home."

Not saying anything, he stood there scratching his head and inspecting his right hand. Kara left him and headed to where she left her bicycle.

"Kara!" Riona flew out of the cottage when Kara was leaning her bicycle against the porch.

She opened the basket and handed her the bubble gum cotton candy. Riona tried to tell her about her day, about how crazy the animals were going, but Kara didn't want to talk to her. Her arms were hurting.

Sean was cooking in the kitchen and called after her but she didn't want to speak with him either.

Kara locked her bedroom door and smoked *krystallis,* then tried to sleep but her arms bothered her. She got a carving knife and was digging into her skin, convinced that there was a sword inside her arm, when Riona came in and screamed. Then Sean drove her to the hospital to be sedated.

She woke in the field tent with braziers burning. The hospital building was full of other people who'd lost their minds as well and they'd set up tents to accommodate the overflow. The Longdark and the prolonged celebration caused many injuries, some fatal. There had been a great fuss with the nurse telling Sean that Kara had died because they couldn't get a pulse. Auntie had to come and explain that it was just her heart condition.

"It hurts all the time," Kara cried to the nurse whom she didn't know.

Sean swore that he was going to find and kill Declan for drugging her. He said that she'd been ranting about white swans. Kara was discharged from the tent so they could give her bed to a man with a twisted leg. He also had a rod lodged through his liver and was carried in on a stretcher.

The drive home was uneventful, and the rest of the day was spent with Kara mumbling about white swans.

"The winter swans come next month," Sean explained, patting Kara's head. "We'll go to Cold Lake and watch them. I'll show you how to boat on the freshwater, all right? Now drink this, it's medicine, and go to sleep. You're frightening Riona, and you don't want to do that, right?"

Kara didn't want to be trouble. She swallowed the herb and went to her room.

The next morning was still dark. Auntie hadn't come home and needed to work extra shifts at the hospital with all the injured. Uncle Sean had to go to work, but with Kara not in the right mind to watch Riona, Sean told the girls to 'pack lunch and get in the car'.

Excitedly, Riona clapped in the car, and whispered, "You're just pretending to be ill, aren't you? Keep doing it. I like going to Papa's work. They have hot chocolate there."

The control tower was tall with spiraling steps and a panoramic view at the top. It was like a lighthouse by the shore and kept a light on so planes knew where to land—they were expecting someone called Francis to return. In the meantime, all everyone talked about was the Raven Queen's death. A vampire had walked out into the sun.

Riona rolled around the floor on a chair with little wheels on the legs, and Kara fell asleep on the sofa in the rest area. She'd been dreaming about a sad boy crying in an iron box buried underground when she felt Sean cover her with his jacket and check her fever.

Don't be so sad, she thought about the boy. *My heart hurts too.*

She opened her eyes when she felt light on her face. Beyond the panoramic window, the sun was setting with a gold hue behind the mountains.

"That's not three days," he heard a man say, not Sean.

"The Ravens are still out?" That was Sean. "Fuck."

"Yeah, man, fuck," said another.

Kara got up and stood by the window looking at how beautiful the Maker's creation shimmered in the warmth of the evening.

That night, Kara and Riona slept in the staff quarters, a single room with bunk beds. Kara woke up at dawn, feeling better. Nothing was hurting or scratching, and the compulsion to dig inside her bones had subsided.

She had coffee with Sean and the four others on shift and learned that the Resurgence had thirty-seven towers. The one they were in was Tower Fifteen. Riona was still asleep.

"There are that many planes, Uncle?" Kara asked, letting her uncle drip a bit of whiskey into her coffee to lift her spirits.

'Spirit' was a pun and a man with black-rimmed glasses laughed about it. Three men and an older woman, they were a jolly bunch at breakfast. But Kara thought that they chattered continuously and laughed to hide their concerns and grief. Every so often, one of them shook his head and sighed. Sean fidgeted endlessly, spinning a pencil in his hand.

Queen Madea had been deeply revered, like Gabriela Arriaga, and they whispered how Francis taking over the Ravens would divide the Ravens and Resurgence because Francis and Mathis couldn't stand each other. More urgently, they were worried about a faraway place called Groom Lake.

"Are there many planes, Uncle?" Kara repeated. "Why are there so many towers?"

"Yeah, fighter jets," said Sean. "We're on an island. The faerie don't sail but they fly. Aerial defense is our best defense." He patted Kara's back. "This one is going to be a pilot."

The older woman gave her the thumbs up. She had a face that liked to smile, and her eyes warmly creased when she did so. A beeping came from one of the monitors, and all swiveled in their chairs. Uncle got up from the table to inspect the noise. "It's Xena."

Everyone exhaled, their postures slackening. "Francis returning so soon?" asked one.

"At least he's returning," said another.

After some minutes of the men standing by the windows with coffee mugs and lifted spirits, discussing the weather and talking about fishing boats, Uncle picked up a receiver and said, "Xena, check your altitude."

The one with glasses bent down to check the monitor. "She's coming in too high."

"Fifteen to Xena, check your fucken altitude. You're going to miss your landing," said Uncle. "Fifteen to Xena, over?"

"Who's flying?" a man with a red beard asked the older woman.

"McCoy," she said.

"Fifteen to Xena, comply and drop your altitude. Or I'm about to blow you out of the sky." Uncle turned and looked at the man with glasses questioningly.

"Alert air patrol and have the Fighters escort her down. Maybe her gear is broken," said the glasses, chewing his lips. "I mean, it's Francis. We don't want to be blowing the Raven King out of the sky."

"He ain't king yet," said the woman.

As Kara watched her uncle work, trying to learn, she had to rub her temple because a white swan was flapping its wings in her mind again. She got up to find her satchel hanging from a hook by the door, fished out her pipe and a bag of *krystallis*, and headed to the washroom.

Kara had been exhaling red mist and losing track of time when there was a bang at the door. "I have to pee!" Riona was awake.

She washed her face before stepping out. Checking her bandaged arm, Kara saw all her self-inflicted wounds were healed but something told her she should hide that. She put the blood drenched bandages back on.

When she returned to the control room, the veins in Sean's temple pulsed as he screamed, "Gear down, Xena! Your landing gear is up!"

Kara walked up to the window, and with her forehead glued to the glass, she watched an enormous plane careen down the runway, clipping a row of parked planes. Sliding on its belly, it continued its destructive path, mowing down trees and upturning earth. The control tower was in chaos by then, but she heard the older woman say, "Hostiles," and turned to her. She was staring at a screen with hundreds of green dots, a clock hand swiping over them.

"Hostiles!" she screamed. "Incoming faerie!"

The shooting began on the runway. From the height Kara was at she thought the earth was moving, but they were lycans. As many ants, they were pouring out of Xena.

Then all the alarms sounded, men screaming into speakers, but it was only morning.

Crucify

Scratching sounds startled Lucien awake. It sounded like a shovel, and he hoped it was a shovel. Then he felt the upward motion. Iron bolts clanked and the hinges creaked as the lid opened and fresh air rushed in.

"Had a good sleep?" Poppy was looking down at him, her doe eyes blinking.

Lucien squinted at the lantern light in his face.

"At least he hadn't pissed himself." Jude, a mousy blonde, another one of Silverfox's, smirked.

Eamon, a man with a single braid from the crown, long and cuffed with gold, and a thick beard, pulled Lucien up. "Come on, boy, let's get going. The night is wasting."

All three were purebloods, and all three were loyal to Silverfox. The constellations shone brightly in the clear night sky, and a crescent moon sat snug above the hills.

"Where is Silverfox?" Lucien asked as Eamon opened the door to Silverfox's black sedan with a gold raven on the hood.

"Raven Keep," Poppy snapped, and opened the driver's door.

The two women sat in the front while the large Eamon and Lucien squeezed in the back. Poppy adjusted the rearview mirror as she did when Lucien was in the car. "Vamperish immortalis, Lucien. Hail the Raven King."

"Where is Francis?" Lucien frowned.

"Silverfox will explain," said Jude. "But my bet is he's dead."

"Groom Lake?" Lucien asked.

"Yep," Jude said. He couldn't see her face in the mirror, only Poppy, but he imagined that Jude bit her lips—a habit that she had.

"Resurgence?" Lucien asked.

"Francis took a single cargo plane with him, Xena," Eamon answered. "A couple of pilots, some human crew, and *all* of his Ravens, full and pure. But the joint operation halted cold when Mathis pulled out. Again, Silverfox will explain."

Lucien didn't know what to make of it. Being surrounded by Silverfox's men was good but it felt wrong. Something was amiss.

An hour later and they were racing dawn, Poppy complaining about how it took hours to find Lucien and hours to dig him up. Silverfox had been adamant that they not travel during the eclipse. A good call, Lucien was informed, as the eclipse had only lasted a day and a half. They'd been looking for Lucien for the duration, and according to Eamon, they'd dug thirteen other holes.

The candelabras set around the room haunted Silverfox's study. It had a desk, a short table, and some chairs. The room used to have tall arched windows, but bolted with iron shutters they looked like a doorway to nowhere. Ella Fitzgerald sang about a shark with pearly whites on a gramophone—'Mack the Knife', Lucien recognized—and Silverfox was as high as a kite, dancing alone.

He kissed Poppy on the mouth when she entered, then asked everyone to step out as he motioned for Lucien to sit. For once the fireplace was lit, and Silverfox settled across from Lucien, crossing his legs and his immaculately shined boots that he never got dirty caught the orange hue of the fireplace.

When the door closed and it was just the two of them in the room, Lucien said, "You grabbed me before Madea opened the door."

"Did I?" Silverfox didn't meet his gaze but was looking down to load his pipe.

"Madea thought someone was coming. She also didn't know it was daylight outside." Lucien had much time to think alone in the dark. The queen had always been gone up there, but not that far, and the only Raven powerful enough to fuck with her like that was Silverfox. "You walked your queen in the sun."

Francis's foresight was a couple of minutes. He was in the room with her when she pulled the door open. He *must've* foreseen what Madea would do but didn't save her. Yet, it was Silverfox who caused it. The queen was undone by those she trusted the most, her bonded.

"So what?" Silverfox lifted his gaze. "I protected the Resurgence. Thank me for all the lives I saved instead of accusing me, Lucien. Her mind was so far gone that she would have approved Francis's assault on Groom Lake."

"You don't care about the Resurgence." Lucien got up and helped himself to a glass of whiskey from the table. "You wouldn't have killed her had she not rejected you."

"I loved her for five hundred years, son. But she never gave me the time of the day. I tried to not hate her when she rejected me and bonded with a human instead. She rejected Francis too, and his hate wasn't so subtle.

I was loyal to her through all her faults, and there were many. I thought having you would help her, ground her mind into reality, but she would rather pine after the dead. And now I've sent her to her bonded.

"When she was young, Madea was glorious. She was a warrior and a goddess, and I worshiped her. But the loss of her mate broke her. For a hundred years I've been carrying her and it's a heavy weight, Lucien."

"Where is Francis?" he asked, drinking the whiskey as if it had been water. He'd been thirsty.

"Sit, Lucien."

He complied.

"The Longdark is a trick of the mind, the same trick Whiteswoon keeps pulling and the same trick we keep falling for," began Silverfox. "The Bloodline War started like the Third Great War, humans killing each other. The great nations depleted their arsenals launching them at one another. In those days, people had stopped burying the dead because there were so many, and a plague ravaged the world.

"Five years, Lucien. The human civilization disintegrated in five years. Once we discovered the otherworldly interference, the conflict became the Bloodline War, and in four and half decades we destroyed the world. Do you know how old I am? I've met King Henry VIII, that is how old I am. I've personally known Anne Boleyn and that is my age.

"But when Madea chose a twenty-year-old human over me, I let her because I wanted her to be happy. But I will *not* let her kill you, do you understand? She would have sent you to Groom Lake. She would have commanded the Resurgence to their deaths.

"The first time Whiteswoon pulled this trick, everyone was convinced that the faerie portal was in Groom Lake. It's a military compound in the lost continent, the place of the first recorded occurrence of the faerie. Destroy the portal and the faerie would magically drop dead was the shared sentiment, and the military minds threw everything at it. A hundred and twenty thousand soldiers lay dead there. A number we couldn't have afforded in a dying and depleting world.

"The second time he pulled the same fucken trick was when Arriaga got it in her head that she'd located the last of the nuclear warhead on that forsaken continent. All the arsenals had been launched in the Third Great War, but she was convinced she'd found a forgotten gem. She went to retrieve it and never returned. The five thousand men she took with her didn't return either.

"Whiteswoon understands men. When one gets it in their head that they are right, they no longer hear reason. I warned Arriaga many times that she was flying out too far from her power base, but she called me a coward. Madea wanted to go with her, and I locked her in the basement. She hated me for a hundred years for not letting her die on a fool's errand.

"A decade ago, everyone just knew there was going to be a three-day-long solar eclipse. Never mind that such a thing isn't possible on this planet. I argued with Madea and Francis many times that it *must* be another trick Whiteswoon was pulling to lure the Resurgence and the Ravens to their final battle.

"I thought I was right, but I *knew* I was right when both Francis and Madea foresaw victory, a full year ahead. That's not possible, Lucien. Whiteswoon had penetrated their minds. Francis got this savior complex and he wanted to be the one to slay the faerie king. That was fine. He was a fool. But Madea couldn't see it either. She was keen enough, always had been, but her hatred for Whiteswoon blinded her. She didn't care who died so long as she got him." Silverfox furrowed his blond brows as he exhaled red mist.

"Ade, Lasso, Orla, Francis, Faidh... your entire covenant, you let them go knowing they'd die?" asked Lucien.

"It was the only way to protect you. I didn't have the numbers because Madea had eroded my authority. And you know what? I don't fucken care. I was furious when they sent you to Nocturne and you nearly died. So I walked my queen in the sun. I killed her brother. But you are here. You matter to me more than them. Is that so bad?"

Lucien didn't know what to feel. His father killed his mother and uncle. Perhaps this was what Kara had felt: confusion of loyalty. But unlike her, he didn't hate his father. For one, he didn't think Silverfox had been cruel. Had the mission really been fated to fail, Silverfox would have saved *thousands* of human lives.

"It's Arriaga, isn't it? The human Madea bonded with..." Lucien asked although he already knew. Their love had been so intense that Kara, Arriaga's daughter, and him, Madea's son, felt the remnant of it a century later and it burned him, nonetheless. It made sense why he pined for Kara so much, but it also meant the feeling wasn't his—the bond had been inherited from his mother.

"Yes."

"There is no portal in Groom Lake?" Lucien asked after accepting the glass pipe from Silverfox.

"There might have been one long ago." Silverfox shrugged. "But it's been closed for at least a century and the faerie still live. When Madea was losing her mind about Arriaga not returning, we went to the forsaken place. It's an abandoned base. In the desert, there isn't any shade in miles. It's a graveyard of the first campaign, skulls buried inside the volcanic ash-like cinder that sinks the boot to the knee with each step, and skeletons of tanks, cars, and machines that men operated." He shuddered.

"Crashed planes and overturned trucks, we proceeded through the night and breached the compound. It's an underground maze. We cleared it by the floor, by each room, but there was no portal, no nest, no Whiteswoon or Gabriela. Madea knows this because she was with me.

"There is nothing at Groom Lake but death. It's not even a lake, it's a salt mine. It looks white from above because it's a salt mound. It's dead lands, Lucien, and Madea would have taken you and the Resurgence to it to die. She knew the eclipse was a hoax, but she would have taken you still because Whiteswoon had called her out and he would have been there. She wanted to kill him, and she would have sacrificed what little was left of the world to avenge Arriaga."

Silverfox clicked his tongue. "Had I been able to, I would have done it with silver and given her a dignified end, but that would have triggered her foresight. Had I come through the door with a knife, Madea would have seen me hours ahead. We all play within the bounds of the talents the Maker has gifted us. She can foresee, I can *weave,* and I'm simply better at the game than she or her brother. But so what? Crucify me."

"How did you find me?" Lucien asked, recalling how Lasso claimed that no one knew where they buried him.

"I know Francis." He smirked. "He's predictable."

"What happens now?" Lucien whispered, staring blankly at the pipe for a long time before lighting it.

"You're the Raven King." Silverfox tapped his heart in a salute. "But I'm the Regent till you're a bit older and a little less kind. Resurgence is mine. I own Mathis the same way you own Sean. Mine just happens to be a general." Silverfox wanted to be king and now he was. He wanted to be free of Madea and he was.

"Vamperish immortalis." Lucien saluted his father and bent to kiss his Raven ring.

To his surprise, Silverfox whispered, "It's not like that," and pulled Lucien by the nape. "You matter to me."

A moment passed like that, where Lucien closed his eyes and let the present be. He didn't worry about the future or gripe about the past. He wanted to believe Silverfox so he wouldn't be so alone, and he let the hopeful sentiment be without prodding at it further.

A cry in the wind, alarms blared from the watch towers, and Silverfox's hand dropped away from Lucien. They both turned to the doorway to nowhere as if there was something to see.

"Hostiles!" Shepard, a pureblood that carried his blade in his staff, burst in. "Hostiles, Silverfox!"

"What hostiles?" Silverfox blinked.

"Faerie," said Shepard.

Lucien flicked a look at the grandfather clock behind the candelabra: eight in the morning, nearly twelve hours to nightfall. For twelve hours, Resurgence was alone.

Looking down, Silverfox was quiet for a long moment, then he laughed. "Well, fuck me."

Three

Protocol

Out through the windows of Tower Fifteen, miles and miles of beautiful valley stretched. Farmlands were divided and colored differently with various grains. White sheep and brown cattle grazed on gold and auburn turf. The horizon was shaped by the peaks and dips of the mountains. The view had been beautiful in the sunset yesterday, but now at high noon, chaos had engulfed it.

A burning jet fell from the sky like a bright leaf twirling on the wind and crashed into a herd of sheep in a fiery eruption.

A chopper was chasing down a group of lycans galloping toward the town, the machine guns strobing orange as they barraged the monsters. Lead didn't penetrate their spiked hide, Kara knew that, but so did they. The assault was meant to slow them down and let the truck chasing them catch up. The chopper dipped low, too low, when the red stream of its flamethrower—which did kill lycans—didn't reach the road. The wake of a jet passing by above, chasing a faerie, blew the flame back into the chopper and a man on fire, a little dark spot, flaked off, falling toward the earth. A lycan leaped on board through the helicopter's open side door and it spun out of control, crashing, and mowing down elm trees with its blade and coming to rest on the pathway of the truck that had been giving chase. The truck veered off-road, rolling over. Lycans piled atop it.

On the runway right below the tower, a lycan punched out the windshield of a jet taking off, and the plane careened into a parked, bigger plane, both catching fire. Kara couldn't keep her eyes off the carnage, but she held Riona with her face buried in her chest. She hummed a song for the little girl because her father was screaming into a speaker right next to them, "Keep them off the Raven Keep, the bastards are all over it!" He'd been screaming for a long time.

"Where is St. Louis?" asked Riona.

Kara didn't know. "Shhh," she padded the girl's back. "It's going to be okay."

A ball of fire like a small sun crashed into the tower's window, shattering all.

"Fae fire!" someone screamed. It was the man with the glasses, and his mouth was open but silent, burning like a wick by the time Kara saw him.

She was on the floor, crawling with Riona. The fire flowed like liquid and flooded after them. Someone yanked her up and she was face to face with Sean. He was yelling, Kara guessed, because his mouth was animate, but her ears rang and she couldn't hear him over it.

They ran down the spiraling stair, around and around as if they were in purgatory and going nowhere. The older woman was with them. Sean had a spear. The woman carried a crossbow, and the quiver on her back was full.

Leaving purgatory, they stepped out into hell. The world was burning silently as Kara only heard the ringing in her ears. The faerie didn't sail and the lycans didn't fly, so perhaps they never thought they'd be facing them at home or perhaps the Ravens didn't allow humans to carry silver, but all their weapons were iron. The woman shot her arrows, getting a lycan in the eye socket, and her second shot pierced the inside of its snarling mouth, but it ate her anyway. Her name had been Camila, Kara remembered.

Sean speared a charging lycan, braced against the impact, and kept him at an eight foot distance as Kara tossed Riona into the back seat of the car. She kept the girl's head down so she wouldn't see the monster swatting at her father.

"Can I open my eyes now?" she asked.

"No."

Kara couldn't drive but she found the tire iron in the trunk and smacked the lycan in the head from behind. Eight-inch quills shot out, spraying her. A hundred needles punctured her skin. The pain was excruciating. Sean dragged her into the car, shoved her inside, and jumped in the driver's seat.

The tires screeched, swerving around the lycan. Neither the spear nor the whack to the head had affected him as he chased their car. That one was male—it had a dangling cock.

Kara yelled with each quill she pulled out. It had a little curved hook at the end that snagged. There was one in her cheek and when she yanked it, a piece of flesh was at the end of it.

"It's venomous. You need an antidote," Sean was saying.

"Don't touch it!" Kara snapped at Riona when the little girl tried to help. Kara didn't need any antidote. She seemed to know a lot of things without knowing why or how she knew them.

"Where are we going?" she asked, pulling a quill out from her inner thigh.

"To pick up Eilis." To avoid the military truck coming head on, he veered off the road and drove on the dirt, leaves flying by the windows.

"Then we're headed to the base. Hold on till then, Kara. Don't fall asleep, you won't wake up."

The town was a wreck as they drove through it. Loudspeakers mounted on poles were yelling, "All civilians head to your nearest shelter before sixteen hundred hours. Protocol Four is in effect. If you're unable to reach a shelter, find a basement and barricade yourselves. I repeat, Protocol Four is in effect. Find shelter before sixteen hundred hours."

"What is Protocol Four?" Kara asked, sliding out a quill from the forearm she'd carved up.

"Air sweep," Sean said, swerving wildly as a burning cow charged through the street. "They're going to bomb the area because we've lost control."

Kara flicked a look at the green clock on the dashboard: 13:15. Then it changed to 13:16. They had less than three hours. "Where do the planes come from?" Kara asked.

"Browndowry." Sean looked at her in the rearview mirror. "The Resurgence's air base is in Browndowry. Why don't you know? Didn't you spend your entire life there?"

Kara couldn't remember. Her father was a watchmaker, a man with a black mustache who liked his tea without sugar or milk, and her mother was a teacher with a long blue skirt and leather flats. They both died in a boating accident that damaged her brain. Other than that, she couldn't remember. Did she have friends? If she did, their names and faces were a mystery. "I don't know, Uncle. My head is not all right."

Sympathy fluttered across his face but as soon as it appeared, it was lost and shifted to fear. Kara followed his gaze and saw a faerie on the road. Wearing full armor, it had a helmet and looked like a metal giant wielding a greatsword that slashed through a car and a man in the same swing. Its wings were taller than two men stacked atop one another.

Sean swerved and drove into an alley. Kara turned in her seat to see the faerie punch a soldier through the head. Brain matter dripped from his gauntlet. His armor had been dark, and an image of a black hat floated by in Kara's mind.

"Are they always so large?" she asked.

"I don't know," murmured Sean, and his hands were trembling as he gripped the steering wheel tighter. "I've never seen one. They haven't crossed the Atlantic in a long time."

A thing Kara should know, she supposed. Something told her that she shouldn't ask too many questions and she shut up.

Fifteen hundred hours and they were still at the hospital. The sick tent was being run over. Lycans were eating the ill and gore oozed from their jaws. Sean couldn't find Auntie Eilis. He was running through the carnage and screaming her name. Kara kept Riona close by, breaking a vending machine to get a chewy candy.

"You sit here." She put her on the bench inside the white brick hallway of the hospital while soldiers with flamethrowers pushed back the lycans beyond the double glass doors. "One bear, two bears, a red and a blue bear, you count the candies as you eat them, all right?"

Riona nodded.

Kara meant to sit down next to the girl to keep her company, but a man was thrown against the glass door, sliding down with a red slime, then the glass warped from heat and shattered. A faerie walked in with his wings folded like a white feathery cloak over his slender body. It wasn't the monster they'd seen in the alley, but a monster nonetheless, his eyes completely black.

Kara picked up Riona and ran as soldiers passed her, firing their rifles. One had a dagger and he'd thrown it, but the knife stopped midair. Kara froze mid-stride and two soldiers, the one who had thrown the knife with his arm extended and the other aiming his rifle, both froze like the mannequins inside a store window downtown. Riona's long hair, red like her mother's, hung in the air from the bounce.

Suderhul, it was fae shadow bind—Kara knew it. She just didn't know how.

The faerie, walking leisurely past Kara and Riona, flicked the cap off one soldier and tilted his chin up with a bony finger.

"Zaluu bas huurhun," *young and pretty,* said the fae. "What a waste." He slid his clawed hand into the soldier's guts and pulled his entrails out. The soldier didn't scream or move.

A light flashed in the corridor, disrupting the shadows for a beat and the gutted soldiers screamed, collapsing onto the floor. Kara lunged forward and had to find her balance again as she smacked into the wall with Riona. The soldier who'd tossed the knife yelled like a cornered animal, flurrying his fists at the faerie's face.

An iron harpoon gored through the faerie's chest. He fell forward, the wings fluttering like a moth caught in a lamp as a soldier stepped on his back. He wrapped a wire around the faerie's neck and with a whirring sound, the wire tightened, slicing off the head. As the soldier rose, signing for his comrades to move forward, Kara saw his painted face and recognized him. He was the soldier Declan had called over to the table. *Redhawk,* he'd boasted, *elite unit.*

He and his fellow soldiers wore a green uniform and a dark beret with a Raven pendant. On his green armband with orange lining, it said, 'Freedom Fighter'. A silver cross dangled from his neck. He didn't recognize Kara and moved on down the hall.

Auntie Eilis was in the basement of the hospital, a cramped space reeking of illness. She was wrapping a bloody baby in her nurse's white robe and passing it for Kara to hold while she put her hand inside the mother, yelling, "The placenta isn't separating."

"Support his neck," Riona instructed because Kara was holding the baby wrong. "He can't hold his head up. Why don't you know?"

Kara handed the baby off to Riona. She didn't know a lot of things she should but knew others that she shouldn't. There was no explanation other than her head injury. For one, she knew the bombs wouldn't do jackshit other than destroy the town because they'd been announcing it all day. Both lycans and faerie spoke the human language. The lycans were keen enough to take shelter, and the faerie, of course, flew.

More than once, she heard a faerie speak in their tongue and she'd understood them when Sean hadn't. Perhaps she was just disturbed and imagining the meaning of the words, and that was the simplest answer.

The baby in Riona's arms was alive and crying but less than ten feet away, a woman was insisting her child was alive when he wasn't.

"He's sleeping," she kept arguing while the boy was blue and had a hole the size of a fist in his chest.

Thunder roared above, the earth trembling as if giants were stomping. The lights in the basement blinked. The walls quaked and plaster fell from the ceiling. It was sixteen hundred hours, Kara guessed.

The structure vibrated till the lights blinked a final time, the room turning pitch dark. People were crying. Then there was a great noise, and Kara breathed a mouthful of dust. Something, a wall or a part of the ceiling, collapsed, and now people were screaming.

Someone knocked her over and a boot stepped on her hand. Kara tried to get up and was knocked back again. Bodies were charging like a herd in the dark, trampling on each other. Kara would have stayed down and covered her face, but she heard Riona and the baby crying. She had to get to them. She crawled, getting stepped on and kicked. She put her hand down on something warm and squishy and yanked it back, wiping it on her dress.

"Riona!" Kara screamed. "Riona!" She'd found the wall and stood up against it. "Riona!"

She couldn't breathe and couldn't see either. She didn't understand why the people were screaming and pushing when there was nowhere to go. "Riona!"

A large male rammed her against the wall. He'd been running in the fucken dark. Tasting blood, rage burned through Kara.

"Riona!" she screamed, and a bright flash burst into the room. Kara's hand was pulsing with it, but no one saw her, because in the light everyone saw the two lycans in the room. Part of the ceiling had collapsed, and they'd burrowed in—the third dropping through the same gap.

As frenzy consumed the room, Kara picked up a brick from the ground. Riona was with her mother, Aunt Eilis hiding behind a metal cabinet and shielding her daughter as a lycan swatted at them.

"Get away from them!" Kara hurled the brick at the lycan's head. It smashed the monster's skull and burst into a dust plume. The sound was as if a gun had gone off. The lycan dropped like a sack but that wouldn't kill it.

The ball of light, the little sun, hovering below the ceiling was losing strength and unraveling. Soon, it would be dark again. She was kicking the door and rattling the hinges but it had no give. Something had collapsed on the other side against the door, and they were stuck. She'd been facing away from the room when claws came out through her stomach—it didn't hurt. On instinct, she turned with a swing and saw she had a blade in her hand when the lycan's head fell off its body. She checked her stomach and it wasn't bad, then the sword was just gone. She didn't know what was happening and couldn't tell if it was *all* in her head. Maybe she was still at the hospital and there were no lycans.

The light died.

"Kara!" Riona jumped on her and wrapped her little legs around her. The girl felt real enough.

In the space drowning in frenzy, Kara held onto the girl and felt her little heart beating. She didn't remember the Resurgence coming or the door opening, but she was wandering around the collapsed halls with Riona when she saw Sean running toward them. His mouth moved as if slowed down, the words garbled and strange.

Blackhunt

They drove through the grey ruins, dust plumes rising and mixing with the heavy fog settling in for the evening. Kara sat beside Uncle Sean who was driving, while Auntie Eilis told Riona the tale of a sleeping princess and the true love's kiss that would wake her. Kara knew the tale and noticed that Eilis replaced the faeries with pixies because real life faeries were neither small nor delightful.

Kara perked up when Auntie stopped mid-sentence.

There was a horde by the tall limestone walls of the military base. People sought shelter asking for help while soldiers fired rifles in the air. Sean couldn't drive through it.

They abandoned the car, and Kara followed him through the crowd, holding Riona. She was stronger than Eilis who could barely hang onto her husband's arm. Aunt and Uncle had trusted Kara with their daughter's life, and pride warmed Kara's chest. She was helpful, she did good, and it made her happy despite all else.

Sean pushed forward holding up his badge and yelling his name and rank, till a soldier saw him, inspected his badge, and let them through.

Inside the walls, the base was a chessboard of beige buildings and white field tents. In front of the largest building protected by two towers, twin flags flew on equal height poles, a green one with a golden clenched fist, and a red one with a black raven. Tanks were parked in the front lawn and batteries with sand-filled sacks and artillery pointed at the sky lined the perimeter.

Soldiers were on edge, pointing their flamethrowers at anything that moved, but they let Sean and his family, including Kara, pass through when he held up his badge. For the first time, Kara noticed that her uncle's badge had a raven on it.

In the hallway with the paint chipping off the walls, neon lights buzzing and flickering overhead, Kara sat on the floor with Riona's head laid on her lap. Men were shouting in the room with a door left open. Everyone was yelling and the smell of antiseptic filled the corridor. Uncle Sean had gone somewhere, and Aunt Eilis was helping in the sick bay while Kara watched over Riona in the corridor.

She dug through her satchel and loaded the last of her *krystallis* into her pipe.

"What does that do?" Riona asked, lifting her tiny head from Kara's lap.

"It calms me down," Kara whispered.

"May I have some?"

"It's not good for little girls."

"Why?"

"It poisons your mind," Kara said, exhaling red mist.

"Then why do you smoke it?"

"To poison my mind."

"Why?" Riona persisted.

"To kill it."

Kara had dozed off. She must have. Riona was wailing. It was so loud with all the other screams and a legless man was crawling toward them, leaving a bloody trail. There were lycans, a horde, in the corridor, crawling on the walls like cockroaches. Kara grabbed Riona and ran.

Gunshots echoed through the halls and plaster flew from the ricochets.

It was night outside as Kara spilled onto the lawn with Riona, but the dark sky was alight with the batteries firing up and the faerie returning fire. Fae fire engulfed men and earth in the liquid flame that stuck to the skin like a heavy coat. She didn't know where Sean and Eilis were and knew she had to get Riona out of there when a lycan jumped and she ducked, holding the little girl. Wings flapped overhead and there were faeries on the lawn—multiple. Dark armored, one of them was the giant she'd seen in the alley.

An explosion knocked Kara off her feet.

"It's fine. Everything is going to be okay," she'd been mumbling, her heels scuffing earth and her sundress catching on twigs and collecting dry leaves as she scooted back, holding Riona.

A beautiful creature, a faerie in white gambeson with golden buckles, pointed his sword tip at Kara. Soft blond locks fell over his perfect face when he snarled, and his mouth and tongue were black. A shadow bind glued her and Riona to the ground, and Kara couldn't toss the little girl aside as the faerie swung at her.

A bright light flashed, disrupting the shadow hold, and Kara twisted as the blade hissed through the air, nicking the skin on her shoulder but nothing more and cleaving onto the earth. The faerie jolted forward as if speared from behind, and that was exactly what it was, there was a Raven pureblood behind him. The blade sliced out through the faerie's neck and arched up, splitting his face in half.

The Raven in a black cloak, black leather gloves, and white curls had others with him—but he was the fastest. Throwing his blade and appearing in time to catch it, he zipped through the front lawn as a blur. The Ravens carried large, square, black shields on their backs, and when someone yelled, "Light!" they ducked behind it as sunlight burst from the faerie in dark armor.

They used the same shield when lycans shot out quills, and they carried a double-edged blade with one edge silver and the other iron—such a blade was called the *reaper*. Kara knew, just didn't remember how as she took Riona and hid behind the thick trunk of an old elm tree.

More Ravens arrived but they didn't have scarlet eyes—fullbloods. The one that kept Kara's attention was the white-haired pureblood, flying through the turf as if he had wings. He double-wielded his blades and mowed down the lycans as if they were tall grass.

The Ravens threw a black orb that looked like an ornament, but when it exploded it flashed. It strobed on the lawn, both from the Raven orb meant to disrupt shadow bind and from the faerie bursting sunlight to burn the vampires.

Ravens piled atop the dark armored faerie, one trying to pull off his helmet. The faerie threw the Raven off him, and his wings spread. Harpoons pierced his wings. Three Raven were dragged across the lawn before the line snapped and the dark faerie flew off.

After a silver lasso wrapped around the last lycan's neck, beheading it with a pull, the yard was littered with the dead. Humans, lycans, and the faerie with their wings stretched out lay alongside each other in a grotesque graveyard. Kara stepped on a faerie's wing and both she and Riona yelped when it twitched.

She recognized the white-haired Raven she'd been staring at as the man who'd come in a black sedan to visit her uncle when he rose with a bloody *reaper* and looked straight at her. His scarlet gaze passed over her as if she was a tree in the orchard.

A man with a black beret and his entourage burst out through the front door, yelling, "Silverfox! Goddamn good to see you!"

"Ten hours till daylight, General Mathis," said Silverfox, turning. "Let's clean up your town before then."

For no reason at all, Kara wanted to go ask Silverfox, *'Where is Lucien?'* The young pureblood who was generous with his *krystallis* had stayed on Kara's mind. But she stopped thinking about him when her heart hurt.

"Come on," she said, taking Riona's hand. "Let's go find your parents."

The fighting continued throughout the night.

A fullblood named Aoife shared her *krystallis* with Kara on the rooftop of the general's complex. Spotlights searched the sky, but the weather seemed to be improving with fewer faeries flying about. Kara had handed Riona off to her aunt and had come out on the roof to take a breather. The hallways smelled like new death, like blood. Come tomorrow it would be old death as the rot settled it. She didn't know why she thought strange things like that, but she accepted Aoife's bowl. Maybe that would help. The wind that was picking up dissipated the red mist from Aoife's mouth.

"Thank you," Kara said, as she took the pipe.

"Mhm."

"Silver or iron?" Kara asked, nodding her chin at Aoife's quiver. Her black shield was left leaning against a ledge but the large bow, like an eagle with its wings spread, was on her back.

"Iron. I'm out here looking for faerie." She tapped the *reaper* on her hip. "The silver is here."

"Where do you live?" Kara squatted down and cupped the flame when her pipe didn't light.

"What do you mean?"

"Where do the Ravens live?" Inhaling diamorphine, she locked her breath for a moment, then came the long exhale.

"You're not from around here, are you?" Aoife frowned.

"No. I moved from Browndowry when my parents died. I'm here with my uncle."

"Who's your uncle?"

"Sean Doyle. He's a pilot."

"Oh, I know him. He flies for the Ravens." Aoife's demeanor relaxed. She took her pipe when Kara held it out to her and placed it in a pouch inside her cloak. "Raven Keep. It's a fortress about fifty miles east of here, a historical landmark too. The locals know. But don't get too close unless you are invited." She winked.

"I'm sorry your queen died."

Aoife shrugged. "She hadn't been well for a long time."

"Do you have another queen now?"

"With time, we'll have a king, Lucien. But he's too young for now."

"Lucien," Kara repeated, tasting his name on her tongue. "What is he like?"

"Lucien? He means well but he's a kid." Lightning quick, Aoife nocked an arrow and followed something across the sky that only she could see, then lowered her bow. "Owl."

"The Raven with white hair, why do you call him Silverfox?"

"It's his name."

"How old are you?" Kara was finding that she didn't know much about the Ravens at all. Probably Riona knew more than her.

"Sixty-seven. I was born here and was Resurgence when I was alive. They say, after a century, you stop counting. But I'm not there yet. We'll see."

Kara nodded. "I would like to see the Raven Keep," she mused out loud.

"You can do that with binoculars." Aoife laughed.

"People are not allowed in your home?"

"Not unless you want to be a meal." Aoife made a snarling face, then pointed at one of her fangs. "Don't forget little girl, Raven Keep is a vampire nest. The treaty holds so as long as there is war, but that seems to be drawing to a close."

"You think so?" Kara wondered.

"The faerie haven't attacked so far from their home base in a century. Something is changing for sure."

It was a long night. The soldiers were mostly out and the fighting sounded distant, a thing flashing and exploding once in a while. The batteries came alive sporadically, loud and mowing down either faerie or lycans, then they'd fall back to silence again.

Aunt Eilis had fallen asleep sitting up and holding a coffee mug, and she didn't wake when Kara took the cup from her. Sean was out fighting, Kara supposed. Jets boomed by overhead occasionally. Although their losses were heavy, Resurgence had been well armed, and Kara wondered why the faerie had attacked at all—especially if they hadn't for a hundred years.

She made sandwiches for Riona in the rest area for the soldiers, a room with wooden tables, empty now that most of them were out on duty.

"Is your arm better?" Riona asked, taking a bite of the ham sandwich.

Kara had forgotten all about it. It didn't bother her at all, and the blood-soaked bandage was just a gory sleeve by now. She was certain it was healed underneath. She nodded.

After the sandwich, they wandered through the empty hallways together. Kara slipped on pooled blood on the floor once, but otherwise, their walk was uneventful. Whatever bodies had been in the corridors had been carried into the morgue.

They saw a large room with an oval table at the center, and two banners, Resurgence and Raven hanging from the wall, and entered. It had chairs with wheels that Riona liked, and the girl had just sat down on one and repelled herself from the oval table, rolling across the room, when a shadow moved from the corner and she screamed. They had missed a seven-foot fall faerie with a ten-foot wing because he hadn't been there. They could bend shadow like that to conceal themselves if they stayed still and if it was dark enough.

Screaming, Riona bolted and ran down the hall. The faerie didn't chase her because he was staring at Kara. It was the one with black armor. He lifted his helmet. He had long black hair and a beautiful face, perfect with a small mouth and sharp nose.

"Judecca," he said.

And a name dropped into Kara's mind: Blackhunt. Then the rest of it came, all of it at once like a dam had broken. She remembered Blackhunt, Whiteswoon, Rosa, all of it. She remembered Lyon, Nocturne, Lucien, and the command he'd left her with.

'If you see Whiteswoon, you will recall him. If you see him or anyone from his court who would recognize you, you will remember yourself and them. It's so you have a fighting chance, Kara, don't resist me.'

Blackhunt reached for her, and Kara stepped back.

"Your father will be pleased to hear you are alive. He thought you'd aged and died like your insignificant mother. But it appears that you take after him in more than one way."

"He's here?" Kara asked, her voice small.

"Yes."

"Why have you come all this way?"

"Retribution." He smiled, his beauty gone when he bared his black teeth. He tried to snatch her, and Kara ducked.

She leaped out of the window and her wings spread. The batteries rattled after her, and when an arrow hissed, clipping her right wing in burning agony, she knew that it was Aoife. If Whiteswoon was here, she couldn't be. It was time to leave, fly away, and find a new home until he came and burned it down again.

The faerie hadn't crossed the Atlantic in a hundred years, but now they had. Something *had* changed and now Kara knew what it was—the Raven queen's death. Whiteswoon used to say that she could foresee far into the future and that she'd see him coming if he attacked.

Blackhunt had explained that it meant that the queen would foresee all possible outcomes with every move and countermove till she found the one that worked. Had Whiteswoon attacked her, because her talent was limited to her surroundings only, she would have found a way to kill him. Because of her, he'd kept his distance, but she was now gone. The Raven Queen's death was the difference.

Soaring into the dark skies, Kara wished she could have seen Lucien one last time and thanked him for keeping his promise. She got to be human and eat a corndog at the fair. She'd seen the Ferris Wheel and ridden it as well, where at the top, a farm boy called Jonah tried to kiss her.

She'd learned to ride a bicycle and had a family who trusted her with their child's life. She got to be happy when she saved others, and she never thought she'd meet so many free humans. As short as it had been, she would always remember it and the beautiful pureblood who'd gifted her the experience. But as a halfblood freak with wings, she couldn't be seen flying around Raven Keep.

All day, the faerie had barraged the keep trying to break in but had failed. The thing was impenetrable, she had to assume, and they'd shoot her down for flying by too low.

Oh well, she thought and flew over the dark ocean as her chest panged as if she had a heart. *Goodbye, Lucien, and thank you.*

Whiteswoon

The ballistas that had been firing all day stopped at nightfall and the Raven Keep fell silent. River Boyne was washing up dead lycans on her banks, and there was a faerie gored through an old elm in the courtyard as Lucien walked the castle grounds with an entourage of fullblood and human guards. They crowded him as if he was king already, but Silverfox had left him behind like a child.

The dark clock tower chimed at an odd hour, half-hour, and Lucien went to inspect it. He found a door left open. It had looked closed but when he pushed, it gave way. A thing fluttered above him, and two archers nocked up, at the gears of the clock, but after a long, hard look, they found nothing.

"All the doors should be locked and manned from inside," Lucien mumbled, echoing Silverfox's orders because he had none of his own to give.

The tower fed into the main keep by a long underground corridor and both the doors were open there as well. Soldiers had been running through the castle and leaving doors open. Just half an hour ago, there had been much commotion when a group of lycans tried scaling the wall after their faerie master was shot down.

Lucien locked and bolted both doors on his way back to the keep. Then he had nothing better to do than to sit idly. He wondered if Kara was all right. He'd rigged the *weave* to undo should she run into someone who would recognize her. The hope was that she either hadn't seen anyone who knew her and was all right, or had, and she had run off, also all right. Communication lines went dead some hours ago and he wouldn't know the state of the Resurgence until Silverfox returned.

By how their jets were still passing by overhead, Resurgence was still in the fight and that was good. He picked up *Inferno* and was reading by the fire in the study when, just before dawn, Silverfox returned. The clock hadn't chimed for six in the morning and Lucien frowned.

The keep began its lengthy procedure of locking down, bolting all openings with iron, and the fullbloods walking the grounds and clearing each room.

Poppy and Jude were in the study as well. Silverfox's gramophone had to be wound like a music box, and the women did that. Soft music started—blues, the kind Silverfox enjoyed. Silverfox was seated across from Lucien, the fireplace in between them.

"How is it out there?" Lucien asked. He set the book aside on a stand by his chair.

"Worse than I hoped but better than I expected," said Silverfox, accepting a drink from Poppy. He unbuckled his weapons belt and held it out to Poppy. "Can you clean and oil them for me?" His *reapers* were dangling from the belt, blood on the scabbards as well as the hilt. Much blood was on Silverfox himself, and the women too.

Lucien looked down at his clean hands.

"Of course," said Poppy, and Lucien heard her rustle behind him, opening chests and drawers.

Jude settled on the carpet with a drink in her hand as she sifted through Silverfox's music collection.

"How did the lycans get here?" Lucien asked.

"Francis's plane," Silverfox said. "The pilots were glamoured to fly back. But the human mind doesn't work as well under control. They crash landed, I hear."

"Francis is really dead?" Lucien stared at Silverfox's hands, and they were also clean. He always wore gloves and they got dirty, but never his hands.

"I sure hope so. We found his head on the plane, inside a wooden crate. They didn't die in the plane but were beheaded elsewhere and their heads brought onboard."

"They?"

"Yes, Francis and his entourage. Ade, Lasso, Faidh, all of them…" Silverfox sighed. He knocked his tongue, then brought his glass to his lips for a large gulp of drink. "We'll hold a service for them and the missing fullbloods in a few days when things settle down a bit."

"By missing, you mean dead." Not a question, Lucien just said so.

"Most likely."

"Have you seen Sean?" Lucien couldn't help himself.

"Yes, I have, and his family as well."

When Silverfox didn't say more, Lucien lifted his gaze and found Silverfox's scarlet eyes narrowed at him, burning like red embers.

"What?" Lucien asked.

That surprised Silverfox. He frowned. "You didn't hear me?" Silverfox asked.

"You didn't say anything," said Lucien. More silence followed.

"You still can't hear me," said Silverfox.

"What are you talking about?" Was he speaking to him telepathically? If so, Lucien wasn't hearing him.

Silverfox's eyes flicked to Poppy on the divan, wiping and oiling his blades. One was on her lap and the other was on the short table in front of her. Silverfox burst up and dashed for his *reapers* but froze halfway. Lucien tried to get up but could not. Poppy had turned to Silverfox, but she remained where she was, half rising and her hand extending to Silverfox with the *reaper* in it. They were across the room from each other. Jude held a glass in her hand. On her feet, she'd been dancing but had stopped in the middle of a turn. Her hems had been swirling and her hair whipping around, when the shadow bind took hold.

"There is only one faerie who can block his ability," a voice came from the corner, the shadow moving. "It's me and he knows it." Whiteswoon stepped out.

A colossus in titanium armor, the floorboards creaked under his weight and the wings brushed the floor like a white cape when he walked. A gauntleted hand brushed Silverfox's face, tilting his chin up. "You're the last of them, and I'll take my time with you. Apollo, Madea, Gabriela, and you, you burned down my home, killed my young, and slayed my queen. All the others are dead now, and it's just you who is left," he said, pausing to study Silverfox. "Let's play a game, shall we?"

Lucien recalled Whiteswoon from Kara's memory, and he'd seen him *become* out of the shadows two beats before he did. For a beat, fear riddled him. For the next beat, he'd reached for a flasher in his hoodie pocket. He had it in his hand but hadn't had the time to throw it before the shadow bound him.

The ball dropped from his hand by the virtue of gravity, not because he moved, and rolled on the floor, coming to a stop at Whiteswoon's feet. Just as the faerie looked down, light burst. Not sunlight, just light that they used to disrupt shadow holds.

Lucien leaped up. Poppy threw the *reaper* at Whiteswoon. Jude screamed, the glass slipping from her hand. Silverfox caught the *reaper* as Whiteswoon sidestepped it. In Silverfox's hand, the *reaper* arched through the air faster than Lucien could blink, but the blade broke on Whiteswoon's gorget. The *reaper* snapped on contact with Whiteswoon's armor, and the force of the impact sent the broken blade flying across the room, punching into the limestone wall like a bullet and lodging inside.

Whiteswoon already had one hand around Silverfox's neck by the time the flasher had gone off and he never let go. With all his pride and fury, Silverfox couldn't free himself from the faerie. Whiteswoon twisted Silverfox's neck to its breaking point, the pain plain on Silverfox's face.

"If you do that again, I'm going to rip his head off." The faerie looked at Lucien with his dark eyes.

Ravens ran in, reacting to Jude's scream, but they bunched by the door, not knowing what to do.

"Holy fuck." Eamon's jaw dropped and his beard looked even longer.

"Let's play a game." Whiteswoon strained Silverfox's neck an inch further. "It's called Capture the Flag, and you're my flag, Silverfox. The sun just came up and you have till nightfall to try and kill me. If you kill me, you win. If I capture you, however..." Whiteswoon paused, a black grin splitting his pale face. "I'll fuck your woman, silver your covenant, flay you alive, and take your child with me and break him for a hundred years.

"Ready?" He dropped Silverfox. "Set." He closed his visor. "Go."

Perhaps Silverfox would never love Poppy as he had Madea. Perhaps his love wasn't worth much since he'd walked his queen into the sun—the reason for their current predicament. Had Madea with two-hour foresight been alive, they wouldn't be trapped inside their own keep with Whiteswoon. All actions had unintended consequences, some more severe than others. But whatever his care had been for Poppy, it was enough for him to hide her with Lucien, the very first thing he did after they ran from Whiteswoon. Silverfox knew he was going to lose.

The rumors about Francis and the queen had been true, as it turned out. There was a secret passageway in Madea's bedchamber, and it led out to Francis's bedroom at the other end of the keep. Francis was dead with his secrets. His men who might have guessed at it were also dead. Silverfox wouldn't speak so indignantly of his queen, so his men wouldn't know it.

'Wait till nightfall, then go,' Silverfox had said as he shoved Poppy and Lucien inside the narrow, dark tunnel where they sat now, holding their breath.

Lucien couldn't see his watch in the pitch dark and the clock tower no longer chimed, so he had to guess at what time of the day it was. High noon, he thought, and that was a long way from nightfall. An eternity to be listening to his heartbeat and Poppy's breathing, both faltering in the long wait. The Resurgence didn't have a habit of disturbing Raven Keep at daylight unless it was Mathis personally coming over, and the human guards manning the turrets wouldn't wonder why the gate wasn't lifting till supper when their shift changed and they dined in the hall.

"You can't hear me," Poppy whispered.

No one could 'hear' each other. All faerie affected Raven talent but Whiteswoon must have a radius that he could block telepathy. Not foresight though, Lucien had seen him.

"He can't hear me." She was crying.

"There are fifty fullblood here and eight purebloods without us. It will be fine. It's a single faerie."

"If that was true, he wouldn't have stowed us here."

Lucien didn't argue. For one, he didn't know how good Whiteswoon's hearing was. He felt the grip of his *reaper,* trying to compensate for having thought a cowardly thing. The waiting was killing. There had been some commotion earlier where men had been shouting, things smashing and footsteps drumming, but it was dead silent now and had been for a while.

Maybe the action had moved downstairs or into a different tower of the fortress—they were all connected through underground tunnels. He waited.

When he thought it was one past noon, he was at the end of his patience.

When he thought it was two past noon, he knew he couldn't wait six more hours, and two breaths after that, he rose.

"What are you doing?" Poppy asked when Lucien nudged her knee trying to step over her.

"Going out."

"Had it been done," said Poppy. "Silverfox would have come for us."

"I know," Lucien said, and pushed the trap door that slid out behind a painting of Queen Rene in Madea's bedchamber.

"I'm coming then." Poppy got up behind him, and in the bit of light that came through the sliding door Lucien turned to see how much she'd been crying.

"Are you sure?" asked Lucien, his voice weak. "I can't protect you." He could only get himself killed.

"Are you serious?" she scoffed and shoved him out of the way. "I'm tenfold better than you."

She wasn't wrong. And Silverfox was a hundredfold better, yet he hadn't returned. If the Raven commander was dead, Lucien wasn't winning any fights, he had no delusions about that. He simply wasn't going to be pissing himself in hiding while Ravens were dying, and that was that.

Hell

Kara left. Then she came back. She couldn't leave. Lucien was the cause of her chest pain, and it worsened the farther she flew from him. It was better to die than hurt so much.

From above, she'd seen the Raven Keep and the river by it, red with lycan blood, dark-furred bodies lining the banks. She'd seen the enormous iron bows in the turrets and on the battlement. Dead faerie were strewn across their lawn on all four sides. She had no hope of going in and sat in the distance, under a leafless and shadeless tree, staring at the keep.

She thought the iron doors would lift at nightfall and the windows might open, and in the dark she might be able to sneak in. How she'd find Lucien inside the nest, she had no idea. For a start, she wanted to know that he was all right. Then she could wait where she was, till he drove out as he did, hopefully. She'd waited a century to have a heart, she could wait for a few days to speak to him. Her heart would never be inside her, she realized, but that didn't mean she couldn't have one. He'd rejected her twice, perhaps the third was the charm. If not, that was all right. She'd watch over him till she knew Whiteswoon had left for good—that was all.

She'd been thinking this and that, and wishing she had her tchotchke hearts for comfort when Blackhunt flew by overhead. Despite the tree having no leaves, he didn't see her because he hadn't been looking for her.

Getting up, she saw him approach the keep unassaulted and land on the battlement. Then he disappeared, probably by entering the turret. Kara flew after him.

A human held the door open for her when she landed. His eyes were glazed over and the other guards on the wall and in the tower looked as if they'd fallen asleep with their eyes open—they were glamoured.

Kara flew into the tower.

Winding tunnels lit by intermittent torches connected the towers of the fortress, but Kara had to trail her hand along the limestone walls and walk by feel when the corridors got too dark in stretches. Her blades, the ones she'd cut her flesh for and didn't find, now freely slid down into her hands. Faerie magic, when one was of blood, was mostly in the mind—Blackhunt had taught her that. It was why she'd thought forgetting herself would make her human, and it almost had.

The tunnel had many iron doors which were closed, but she'd followed the open ones and came out into a kitchen. The tiled floor was slick with blood and Blackhunt's boot prints led out of the room and down the hallway. She followed the wet red impressions on the dark wooden floor. Hard to see but there were plenty of candles and lanterns lit.

Aoife lay by a door to a library, her face looking up while her body was separated by an inch and turned down. Another dead lay beside her, a pureblood with one red eye, the other missing along with half of his face and the rest of his body. Around the corner, soot darkened the limestone walls and charred bodies lay on the floor. Kara followed the red prints further. Blackhunt hadn't silvered them. The blood was coagulated. They'd been dead for a while. Whiteswoon was here in the keep.

She didn't have courage because she never had fear, but a familiar thing unsteadied her nerves—anger. And she shook with it.

Severed heads on the floor, on the chairs and the long wooden tables, and one body was tangled in a grand chandelier made of bones as she passed through a dining hall. The red prints were thinning and breaking in parts, then disappeared altogether in a carpeted hallway. But by then it no longer mattered, because she heard Blackhunt and Whiteswoon speaking, one of them laughing.

The impulse she had that made her want to pull Vitali's heart out through his throat and chew it raw now pounded through her in lieu of a heartbeat and she let it overtake her. All the wrath and hate inherited from Whiteswoon she let flow through her freely. If he'd silvered Lucien, she'd see the end of him. If he'd taken her heart, his immortality would cease today.

In a grand hall with granite pillars, a mirror above the black throne reflecting the firelight of the hall and concentrating it to appear as if the sun was rising behind the throne, Blackhunt was lounging on the dais with his blade laid across his lap—he'd been the one laughing.

The Ravens crowded the hall in various poses like statues. Whiteswoon was making a show of it. The vampires were aware but unable to move. Glaring eyes, some red and some not, followed Kara silently as she weaved through the hall of dolls, approaching the throne where she heard Whiteswoon.

Silverfox was pinned to the granite floor with *reapers,* probably his own, nailed through his hands. He was moving and conscious as Whiteswoon had his back flayed open. A soft cry fell onto the floor when

Whiteswoon pulled out one of his ribs through his open back and tossed it as if he had a dog to feed. Silverfox was controlling his breathing much like Lucien did, to control the sensation of pain.

"Where are they?" asked Whiteswoon. "Your bastard and your whore?"

Silverfox didn't answer. When his scarlet gaze, darkened with pain, locked with Kara's, a red tear crossed the bridge of his nose.

"Avaa," *Father,* Kara called.

Both Whiteswoon and Blackhunt shifted their gazes to her.

"Amid baih nee," *she lives.* Whiteswoon rose with a smile.

"I told you so, King." Blackhunt didn't bother getting up and laughed, dropping his gaze to Kara's blades.

"Where is Lucien?" she asked.

"Who?" Whiteswoon tilted his head.

"The Raven King."

"He's the Raven King." Whiteswoon stepped on Silverfox's neck and Kara heard the bones crush. As long as it wasn't separated from his body, the injury would heal.

"There was a boy. Have you silvered him? Is that what you've done?"

"You talk much for a bastard child of a slave." Whiteswoon strode for her.

"That's not true. Her name was Gabriela Arriaga and you killed her because you were afraid of her."

Whiteswoon had a double-edged straight greatsword nearly as tall as him, and it came at Kara, arcing through the air. Blackhunt carried a narrow longsword and both weapons were two-handed. The faerie carried the weapon that most suited them, and although Kara's twin blades were a little longer than a short sword and curved, hers were attached to her on a chain. She threw one, the chain wrapping around Whiteswoon's greatsword, and the other flew at the mirror above the throne. She let the chain go on that one.

Her throw was good. It was always good. The mirror shattered. It changed the light and shadow composition of the room.

Over thirty Ravens had been in the hall, and all lunged at once. Some of them were faster than others and were a blur when they moved. They piled onto Blackhunt as Whiteswoon and Kara flew around the hall, crashing into pillars as an entwined mess, wings flapping, claws trashing each other. Whiteswoon slammed her onto an arched window barred with an iron shutter with force enough to dislodge the shutter and break all that was in her. But her heart wasn't inside her. He couldn't break that.

"I hate you more than you hate me!" Kara yelled, the chain of her *Nar* blade wrapping around his neck. The sword she'd thrown at the mirror was lost.

"But I'm stronger than you." The chains broke, scattering on the floor like beads of a pearl necklace.

He punched her into the iron shutter till it became loose from the wall and crashed down into the hall.

Sunlight rushed in. But constrained through a single, tall but narrow window, it was a beam that divided the hall. Vampires parted away from it, and she saw Blackhunt trying to reach the light, a blonde woman on his back, stabbing down at his neck and head with blades in both of her hands. A silver lasso around Blackhunt's neck pulled him back into the darkness, where he continued to grunt. Sunlight flashed but was directed down, Blackhunt's arms bolted to his body.

Kara tangled herself around Whiteswoon, trying to keep him away from the Ravens but he landed on the stone floor, cratering it, with his knee on Kara's sternum.

'Do you think you breathe air?' Blackhunt had asked. *'Is that why you're panting?'*

No, I'm Whiteswoon's daughter and I don't breathe. We're both monsters that the Maker loathes.

With a burst, she took him through the wall and they flew through the keep, plaster flying, bookshelves falling and limestone slabs splintering, but he was dressed in enchanted, impenetrable, titanium armor and she was wearing a white sundress with yellow flowers.

"This gives me more pleasure than you know," said Whiteswoon, his gauntlets closing around Kara's neck as she kicked fruitlessly under him. "It's like killing Arriaga twice. Thank you."

"So you do know her name."

Kara kicked and kicked but he'd mounted her, and she was wrinkling the carpet but not doing much else. Her blade ripped from her and her arms bleeding, she didn't have the physical strength to pry his hands open.

"You're human," said Whiteswoon. "You need air. Now choke."

Stuck, Kara battled the dark waves that threatened to pull her under. If she lost consciousness she'd die. The reason he wasn't tearing her head off was that he enjoyed killing slowly.

Kara was halfway to meeting the Maker when she saw a blur behind Whiteswoon's shoulder. But even as a shape in her failing sight, she would recognize Lucien. It was his eyes. She *loved* how they were large, kind, and saw beauty when there was none.

Whiteswoon didn't have his helmet on, and when Lucien grabbed a handful of Whiteswoon's long, white hair, locking his head in a fixed position, the Raven was touching the faerie's crown. He'd wrapped his legs around Whiteswoon's ribs, locking his heels. Lucien was half his size but he was mounted on his back, between the fae king's wings that flapped wildly all of a sudden. He let go of Kara and tried to elbow back at Lucien, but he was too large, wearing heavy armor, and his own wings were in the way. His movements slowed as his eyes rolled back.

"Kara, go!" Lucien yelled while Whiteswoon was trying to buck him off, flying into walls and the ceiling.

Kara rolled over and coughed, her lungs burning because she was more human than faerie—maybe. Fae magic did tend to be in the mind.

"What are you doing?" she asked because Whiteswoon was swinging at nothing. He'd forgotten about Lucien on his back and was fighting the demons in his mind.

"Weaving the death of his wife, his queen," said Lucien, his scarlet eyes cold and focused. "But I can't hold him forever. You'd better go now, Kara."

It was a *grand* feat to hold Whiteswoon's mind for any length of time, but forgoing that, Kara asked, "Why?"

"So you can live."

While the faerie king was knelt from the weight of a boy half his size and slumped over, Kara reached and touched the side of Lucien's neck and his heart pulsed into her hand.

"I see," she whispered. "That's how it feels. Thank you."

Kara pried Lucien's hands away from Whiteswoon and pushed him off, her shadow bind taking him when he stumbled back. She embraced Whiteswoon, hugging him as tight as a loving daughter would, lifted him with her wings spread, and they flew back through the holes they made in the keep's walls. The slumped over Whiteswoon was a great weight but Kara carried him and flew out into the sun through the broken shutter.

Fifteen hundred feet she climbed straight up, heading to the Maker's endless blue home.

At seven thousand feet, she was looking down at the clouds.

At fifteen thousand, she boomed like a Resurgence jet breaking the sound barrier.

Above twenty thousand, she could no longer breathe.

At forty thousand, Whiteswoon began fighting her. He was breathless just like her—*you're not immortal after all.*

Three-hundred and sixty thousand, and they were both burning from the sun's radiation. Whiteswoon's armor heated to red hot, and his mouth was open but if his scream had a sound, it was lost behind.

At two million feet Kara lost count and sense. Weightlessly, they floated in the frozen void. Terror and pain were sensations new to Whiteswoon, he hadn't had the time to adjust, but this was how Kara lived. Ever since she could remember, all she felt was pain. Not in the body but in the mind, and that hurt worse because it didn't heal. Wrapping her hands around Whiteswoon's wings, her knee in between his shoulder blades, she tore them off his back. She wasn't stronger than him, of course not, she just had more awareness was all. Facing death hadn't stunned her as it had Whiteswoon. Because unlike him, she was willing to die.

Shadow bind the sun, Father. She kicked him toward the ball of fire, and the momentum launched her back toward the earth. If there was hell, it would be on the sun for it was always burning.

"Judecca," she heard him in her mind. *"I'm your father."*

"Travel through your hell alone, Father."

She fell back onto the earth and burned when gravity found her. But she had Whiteswoon's wings in her hands, a thing she'd won, and she laughed wildly while she fell, on fire.

Forever

Kara recalled floating in the salty ocean for days, thinking she was a jellyfish. She remembered being on a boat, the captain saying that he'd followed the shooting star and found her. She did not remember being taken to the Raven Keep, but the windows were boarded when she woke up in a dark room with a lantern on a wooden chest in the corner. There was a wall-mounted dull black mirror opposite her and she was lying on a simple mattress on the floor.

Lucien was seated on the floor not far from her, leaning his back against a wall and reading in candlelight. She didn't see the cover of the book because it was on his lap and his scarlet eyes were looking down.

Her wings were black from being burned and when she stirred, her right wing flailing up inadvertently, Lucien's gaze lifted. She had an ivory silk blanket over her and was dressed in cotton sleepwear underneath. It wasn't cold or hot, just the perfect temperature to sleep in all day or night.

"Do you know who I am?" he asked, folding his book and setting it aside.

"You're Vitali," said Kara, and watched as his soft brows furrowed in concern. She burst into laughter. Tears ran down her face. She cried when she was happy, she was learning.

Lucien wasn't sure that she hadn't lost her mind and came over to press his hand on her forehead. "Your fever broke. That's good. Would you like something to eat? Soup, perhaps?"

"I want *krystallis,* Lucien." She sat up, her fugly black wings rising with her. "Am I in the Raven Keep? Are they waiting for me to get better before they silver me?" she asked as if she was a vampire and as if silver would hurt her.

"You saved everyone's life, including my father's. No one is complaining that you're here."

"Your father?"

"Silverfox. He's our leader... for now."

"You look much like him," she said, now that she'd noticed—same eyes and the same nose but different mouth and hair. They were both lean and built with nearly identical frames. The reason she couldn't take her eyes off Silverfox on the front lawn of the general's compound was Lucien. "Where is Blackhunt?" she asked.

"The other faerie? His head is on a pike above the front gate."

He had been kinder than Whiteswoon, Kara remembered, but that wasn't saying much and there was no grief.

"Here." Lucien held out a loaded pipe.

His hand was warm when Kara's skin brushed against his. His gaze dropped to her mouth.

"You have to know something, Kara," he began. "My mother and yours were bonded. That's why we have a connection, but it's not ours."

That sounded like he was rejecting her again and it made her sad. The pang wasn't Gabriela's but hers. "Is that what you think?" she asked.

"I don't know."

"I smell like smoke, fire, and salt," Kara said. "Is there a bath here?"

"Of course." He got up. "I'll have water heated for you."

"Where is this?" She looked around at the odd collection of human trinkets arranged and spotted her 'Be Happy' heart among them.

"My room."

"Your room?" She glided her hand on the mattress. "This is your bed?"

"Yes."

"You sleep on the floor?"

"I like it better," he said.

"Why?" she asked.

"No monsters under the bed."

"There are always monsters, Lucien."

"That's fine." He smiled. "I just don't want them under my bed."

A moment passed in silence before Kara broke it. "The bath?"

"Yeah." He cleared his throat. "Give me a moment." He stepped out.

The washroom was beautiful with little colorful tiles on the floor like a mural and the images of knights and dragons on stained glass dividers flickered in the candlelight. Kara washed her wings, but the black wasn't soot and didn't come off. They were permanently darkened. She stowed them on her back as ink and had been soaking in the copper tub when there was a knock at the door. The blades in her arms pulsed. Whiteswoon may have ripped them out in a fight, but they were part of the things she carried, like scars, and had returned to her.

"Yeah?" she asked, thinking it may be one of the Ravens.

And it was one of the Ravens. She sometimes forgot that Lucien was a Raven, the most important one for that matter. "I brought you towels," he was saying but dropped them on the floor when Kara got out of the bath to get them.

He turned bright red and stared at her. Then, he blinked and began collecting the towels from the floor, apologizing. He flicked another look at her from the floor and then looked to the side, holding out the towels. "I'm sorry, I didn't realize," he was saying.

"That I'd be naked in a bath?"

"Sorry."

She took the towels and wrapped one around herself. Water dripped from her wet hair and ran down her shoulders and chest. "It's all better now," she whispered.

He turned to her, but the deep blush remained on his face, neck, and the part of his chest she could see, a little spot right between the collarbones. She liked it, the curve of his collarbones, and traced her finger along the fragile line. He didn't turn away from her and held her gaze, then leaned in and their lips met. His heart raced wild, and she felt each beat as if it was inside her.

"I'm fucken dying," he whispered when she broke the kiss because the rush had overwhelmed her.

Having a heart was an awful ordeal for it made her nervous. Where it used to be an empty space, now a hectic thing fluttered. She checked her pulse but it wasn't her. She felt his. They shared a heart.

"I think we should go check your mattress. Perhaps there are flat monsters under it."

"You think so?"

"Better to be sure."

His room was down the hall, a handful of closed doors away in a dark corridor. "What time is it?" she asked. It had been one of the first things she'd asked when they met.

"Around ten in the morning," he said. He wasn't wearing a watch. "We're fixing the clock tower, but it may take a while since each part has to be custom made and fitted. An enormous faerie stuck himself in there and broke it."

He was shy and stood there staring at the floor after he closed the bedroom door.

"What is the dull mirror for?" Kara pointed to ease his discomfort.

He followed her hand with his gaze. "It's a television. Do you want to see a film? I can start..." He trailed off, the last of his words spoken into her mouth when she kissed him and pressed herself against him. His breathing was controlled as if he was in pain.

"Are you all right?" she asked.

"Yeah." His gaze stalked her mouth. He became unstuck from the wall and followed her to the center of the room.

The spot rug was soft wool, and Kara's bare feet sank into it. He wasn't wearing his blades, but he had a belt and she started with that, gently unbuckling and sliding it out through the loops. It dropped on the rug. The buckle didn't make a sound. He wore a white T-shirt, cotton and clean when she touched it and pulled it off over his head, his brown locks falling unruly over his face after the collar of the shirt passed over them. That dropped on the floor as well. He unlaced and took off his shoes. The soles of them were spotless as he tossed them across the room.

He was nervous. The way he reacted to anything she did with total amazement at the sensation, like how he took a lung full of air when she slipped her hand inside the waist of his jeans and glided it across his stomach... it was his first time.

So sweet, he was so incredibly sweet. The way his eyes ballooned in surprise when she straddled him and took him inside made her gasp. She enjoyed his reaction. Although she was slow and gentle in riding him, his breathing soon stuttered. His hands were on her hips, and they clamped down holding her in place, asking her to stop, to give him a moment to recover. She did.

She bent and kissed him, beginning to rock a bit, not too much though.

"Kara, wait." He tipped his head back. "I... I'm not... am I pleasing you?"

She traced her thumb along the arch of his brow. "Come as you want, Lucien. I want you to."

She could have roughed him up a bit and gotten what she wanted, which was to watch his climax, but that would come anyway. She wouldn't vie for control. It was his first time and she let him enjoy it for as long as he could stand it.

He was biting his lips, then grabbed her and flipped her over, landing on top of her. He thrust into her deeper. Kara fought the urge to close her eyes and surrender to him because she wanted to watch him.

When it became too close to call, Kara yanked the control rein, and commanded, "Lucien, come. I want to feel it."

She pulled him down by the nape and held him there. Kept his mouth on hers, as her legs wrapped around him. Now, she controlled him but lost herself, squeezed her eyes shut, and let out a cry, arching into him. She had a fistful of his hair and twisted it. She didn't know if she was hurting him, but maybe not, because his warmth pulsed into her. His chest was pressed against hers, and she felt *her* heart pounding as she was coming.

It took a moment, but eventually, she realized she was still pulling his hair, and dropped her hand, laughing.

The rest of the day was spent with Lucien trying to 'get better', his words.

"Are you all right?" he asked her often and what he meant was, "Am I hurting you?" but there was nothing he could do that would hurt her, except die, and she would *never* let that happen.

Much was yet to unfold. Although Whiteswoon was gone, along with his favored general, the faerie weren't, not by a long shot. They'd only brought a plane full of lycans, yet a continent of them awaited. Nocturne wasn't the only Blood den, she'd heard of others around the mainland, and by trying to kill the Raven heir, they'd started a war.

There was also the rebuilding of Summerset and Greenwillow after the bombing, and Kara did mean to be a Resurgence pilot, but she didn't need a plane to patrol the air. And most immediate of all, she was yet to meet the Raven covenant as a halfblood faerie. She was inside their home, in the bedroom of their heir and they weren't trying to kill her, and that was a good start.

Toward the evening, after the candles had burned out, Kara sat on the mattress with a pipe in her hand—old habits died hard—and watched a film, her first ever, while Lucien slept behind her.

Kara gasped at the TV, her hand over her mouth, and Lucien stirred behind her. All the singing and the dancing and the bright colors, as well as Kara's dramatics, were disturbing him, she thought. "Are we being too loud?" she asked about TV and herself.

"No." Moaning, he turned. "Aren't you tired? You should sleep a little."

Not wanting to explain how the faerie naturally slept less, she only said, "I'm fine, go back to sleep."

But she was shaking him awake soon after. "Lucien!"

"What happened?"

"The wizard is a fraud. He gave the tinman a tchotchke heart!"

"It's okay." He smiled, sleepy. "He had a heart all along. Now, sleep. At midnight, we have to be at Raven Court." He got up to turn off the TV and pulled her as he lay back down.

But then instead of sleeping they lay face to face, Kara studying the sharp peaks and soft curves of his body.

"You're beautiful." She'd made him blush. "Are you mine?" she asked. "Is that what bonded means?"

"Yes."

"Are you bonded to me?"

"Most certainly," he said, kissing her hand.

"For how long?"

"Forever, Kara."

"That's a long time," Kara whispered. "What if you change your mind?"

"I'm not able to, not that I'd want to." He ran his fingers through her hair. "Once I make the initial decision, which I have, the commitment is forever."

"What if I'm bad to you?" Kara frowned. She didn't like that he didn't have free will.

"Are you going to be... bad to me?"

"Never," she promised.

He kissed her and any potential for sleep escaped them both.

Happiness

Kara liked sequins and that hadn't changed. Out of the many beautiful things that were presented to her by Delfie, her handmaiden according to the fullblood herself, Kara chose a short black sequined dress with long sleeves but an open back. It had a slit on one side that came up to the top of her thigh. She also picked black genuine leather high heels.

"We're going to get along so well." Delfie was excited. "How do you want your hair done?"

"It's fine the way it is." Her hair was short enough that she'd wear it down.

She'd been assigned a bedchamber and it was bigger than Lucien's, although that may have been intentional on the Raven heir's part. She had a four-poster bed with a red veil, which she loved, and a beautiful wool carpet. She could say that now, loved, because she had a heart.

She stood looking at herself in a full-length mirror while Delfie applied oil that smelled like lilac to her hair.

"Don't worry, it won't be greasy," she reassured. "But it'll make it smoother." The blonde part of Kara's hair was fried and frizzy.

"Where's Lucien?" Kara asked, flicking a look at the oak door in the mirror.

"With his court." Delfie smiled, fiddling with Kara's hair. "There," she finally said, taking a step back to see her work, then nodded, satisfied.

"I don't know anyone." The trouble with a heart was that now she was nervous. "Will you go with me?"

"Of course."

"Do you have *krystallis*?" She needed to cut out the habit at some point. She should eat food rather than smoke blood, and most of all, she shouldn't be high if she meant to protect Lucien. But just for the night, she thought.

"Of course."

Delfie brought a whole baggie's worth but in a glass vial and charged Kara no *dinne*. A dangerous thing, diamorphine was now free—she would have to watch herself. She thought she indulged only a little, but half the baggie was gone before she realized and it had fucked her mind enough for her to think wearing her new black wings like a cloak would be pretty. After all, in the nest of Ravens, she was the only one with wings.

Delfie jumped away from her, hid in a dark corner, and hissed like a feline. She wouldn't stop hissing till Kara stowed away her wings. Kara apologized but Delfie refused to accompany her to court and requested she find another handmaiden. The wound was too fresh and the war was a long way from being done. In hindsight, Kara didn't know why she'd thought that would be a good idea. Maybe it was best that she didn't smoke anymore.

Kara walked alone through the hallway, the knock of her heels echoing. Grand chandeliers hung from the high ceiling and statues of armored knights as tall as three men guarded the pillars with the black on red Raven banner hanging from them. She could hear the party in the courtyard, the first public gathering Ravens were holding in a *long* time, she'd been told.

The iron shutters were lifted to the courtyard, and the night draft running through the castle gave Kara goosebumps. Beyond the door, the trees were dressed with hanging lanterns, and laughter and music rode the breeze that was cold on her skin. Human children dressed as knights and princesses ran around with sparklers and wooden swords, Ravens were in their black cloaks, and Resurgence wore their green uniform. A pureblood saw her, a woman with large eyes, and weighed her up and down with scorn on her face.

I can't do this.

Kara turned and was face to face with Lucien. He was wearing a black blazer which he took off to drape over Kara.

"It's late fall." He smiled.

"She hates me," Kara whispered, pointing with her eyes at the pureblood with folded arms and a sneer.

"That's Poppy. She hates everyone." He took her arm. "Let's go."

Kara didn't move and he looked back. "Is it okay if I don't want to?" she asked.

"Of course," he said, leaning in to comfort her. His skin smelled good. "Sean is here with his family." He placed his chin on her shoulder as she buried her face onto his chest, probably screwing up his white shirt with the makeup she tried to put on. "Riona's been waiting for you. Do you want to go say hello to her, and then we'll leave?"

Kara nodded.

Lucien stepped back so they'd be face to face. Her heels were tall enough that they were the same height. "Just remember," he said as he took her hand. "You're the most powerful creature here. They know it. They're just trying to see if you do as well. Ravens are a bunch of bitches. They might gossip and look at you weirdly, but so what? Do you really care?"

"Do you?" Kara asked.

"I don't give a damn."

She believed him and let him lead her out.

The air was incredible outside, and Kara relished the moment, in awe at how beautiful the Maker's creation was.

No sooner had she stepped outside than a little girl saw her and sprinted. "Kara!" She didn't care about faeries, vampires, and bloodlines and jumped on Kara, wrapping her little legs around her. "You have wings!" Riona exclaimed. "You can fly like Papa!" The next question was, "Can I fly with you?"

"Sure." Kara set Riona down, glad that she'd come out.

General Mathis, lieutenant that, captain this, lots of important men were introduced to her, and they all wanted to know if she could help train soldiers in 'simulated battles'. It would save lives, Kara heard, so she agreed. The general shook her hand and his wife smiled at her. This wasn't so bad.

When Kara stepped off the pebblestone walkway, her heels sank into the soft earth of the courtyard so she took them off and dangled them from her fingers. The lawn felt pleasant under her bare feet. Lucien kissed her hand and went to get her a drink. Ravens distilled their own whiskey, he proclaimed and insisted that she try some.

Music had been playing the entire time. Kara didn't see any musicians, and besides, from the grainy sound she thought they were human recordings centuries old. Moving slowly to the music, smiling because a song with an attitude came on, a woman proclaiming, *some of these days, you're going to miss me, honey,* Kara tipped her head back and saw she was under a parasol of light. The branches of the elm were wrapped with stringed bulbs.

"So, what are Blood dens like? Are they as revolting as I imagine them to be?"

Kara tore her gaze from the parasol and the Maker's star-studded home beyond and found Poppy with her head cocked. "Next time, tell the seamstress you need a few more yards of fabric," she said. "It's not expensive but if you couldn't afford it, I understand."

"You're welcome to not look at me," said Kara and gestured around the courtyard. "There is much else to see."

"But you are in my keep, aren't you?" Poppy's lips twisted to reveal her fine white fangs.

"If it is *your* keep, you are welcome to kick me out."

Poppy hissed like a venomous snake, but she stopped when Silverfox came up behind her. She cleared her throat and plastered a smile on her face.

"Trouble?" Silverfox asked.

"Of course not." Her smile changed from pretentious to genuine as Silverfox caressed her face with his gloved hand.

"Will you give us a minute?" he asked.

Poppy curtsied to him, lifting the lace hem of her black dress, then strode off.

"Where is Whiteswoon?" Silverfox asked, sipping from a glass of whiskey he held.

"On his way to the sun," Kara said. "I carried him out of the atmosphere, high above the Maker's home, and shoved him toward the sun. He will get there, eventually."

"He can't fly back?"

"Not without his wings. I tore them off and faerie wings don't grow back."

He set his drink on a tray of a server passing by, reached into a pouch in his cloak and took out a glass pipe. After loading it, he held it out to Kara.

"Is it clean?" she asked.

"No."

"No, thank you," Kara said. She summoned fire on her palm when Silverfox's lighter blew out in the wind.

"Neat trick," he said, holding his glass pipe over her fire and rolling the bowl gently.

"Not a trick. It's magic."

He took a moment to hit his pipe, then asked, "You're Arriaga's daughter?" exhaling red mist.

"Yes."

"If you're anything like your mother, you're a fighter. If your allegiance is with the Ravens, we'll get along famously. If not..." he clicked his tongue.

"My allegiance is with Lucien," Kara said blatantly. "If you don't mean to betray him, we shall get along famously."

"He's my son."

"I'm Whiteswoon's daughter. Familial relations mean little to me."

They narrowed their eyes at each other till Silverfox chuckled, appearing warm. "No, girl, you're Arriaga's daughter."

"I never knew her." That was her truth. She'd always been under glamour even before Kara was born.

"I did," he said. He grabbed fresh drinks from a tray when a server passed by. "Lucien's very young, and he's too kind to command during a time of war."

"I agree."

"He's meant to reign over peace, so protect that kindness in him. But so long as there is war, I'm better suited for it."

"I agree."

"Getting along famously already?" Silverfox tipped an imaginary hat and walked away.

Lucien had appeared with a tray of small glasses. "What was that about?"

"Nothing," said Kara. "What are these?"

They were samples of whiskey and Lucien proceeded to explain the different ingredients, distillation process, and aging... he even talked about the barrels they were kept in. Kara found one that was older than her and tried it. It was odd like smooth fire, smoky but had a hint of vanilla.

Then she proceeded to sample all the others. Why not? No one was charging her a single *dinne*.

The music changed, and Lucien took her hand. "Would you dance with me?"

It sounded like a feather floating on a bit of draft. Kara didn't know how to move to such sounds.

"It's just a waltz," he said, the lantern lights twinkling in his red gaze as if the constellations lived inside him.

"I don't know how. I'll look stupid."

"To whom?" he asked, leading her to the center of the courtyard and wrapping his arm around her waist.

Everyone else was staring at them. The one called Poppy was with a group of women and they were sneering at her, but as the music picked up, Kara decided she didn't give a damn and kissed Lucien at the center of it all.

When dawn's cool light broke and it began to drizzle in the courtyard, the party dissipated. Sean came to say hello and she hugged him, lifting the man off his feet.

"It's strange," he said, after she let him down. "I remember having a sister and I remember you being this little." He illustrated a little girl's height with his hand. "I know it was Silverfox's *weave*, but it's real enough. You're welcome in my house anytime you want."

"Thank you!" Kara exclaimed and she meant to visit him *every* day during the sunlight hours. Faerie naturally slept less, and she didn't want to be cooped up in the Raven Keep during the day. She wanted to ride her bicycle, go to town, and train with the Resurgence.

As the last of the guests left, the Ravens locked their doors and bolted their iron shutters. And Kara ran up the stone steps barefoot, laughing. Lucien was after her. For once, she didn't need a tchotchke heart to remind her to 'Be Happy'.

In her bedchamber with a four-poster bed, the red veil draped over, she playfully called Lucien as he entered after her and closed the door. A lantern was already lit for her and placed on the nightstand. She pulled Lucien's shirt, ripping the buttons on the front. Who had time for buttons when they were burning as she was?

Her black sequin dress was on the floor, and she'd been wearing nothing underneath.

"Do you trust me?" she whispered, as his fangs grated down her neck, carrying his warm breath.

"Yeah."

"Lie down, then." She pushed him onto her bed.

Kara stripped the tassels of her heavy black curtains, the window beyond it boarded with an iron panel, and tied Lucien to the sturdy posters of her bed, one wrist at a time. Taking her time, she pulled off his belt, then slowly, peeled his pants down inch by inch. He was squirming already, clenching his fists and releasing them. He had a soft brown trail on his belly, leading to where he was erect. His knee jerked when she rolled her tongue down his length.

"I'm going to die," he whispered, his breath already short.

No, he wasn't going to die. But he was going to become undone for her over and over with each new thing she did to him.

"I fucken love you," he was saying, and she'd test that all day, taking him to the edge and bringing him back.

She didn't have to be gentle either, it wasn't his first time.

They'd spent the whole day and half the night like this, and Lucien shivered when Kara touched him between the shoulder blades. They had a bath together where more of the same ensued, and at some point, Kara had lost herself and her black wings spread. They were on the ceiling. He didn't care because he was coming, and she was too.

On the second day, she woke him before dawn. "I'm going to go to the Doyles's, all right?"

"Why?" he frowned.

"I want to get out," she said, kissing his sleepy brow. "I'll be back by nightfall."

He pouted but let her go. He was too tired.

Delfie returned, apologizing for overreacting. As Lucien slept on her bed, Kara washed her face, picked out her new attire, a deep green dress like pines of fir, found white flat-soled shoes with laces, and hopped on a bicycle she borrowed from one of the guards.

She promised to bring Delfie back a gallon of ale, and a bottle of whiskey from Devon for the guard whose bike she borrowed, and then she pedaled away to Summerset.

Riding through the woods thick with fog, morning dew glistening on the forest floor, the songbirds already chirping, calling each other and the world to say hello, Kara let go of the handlebars and felt as if she was flying. She could take to the skies, of course, and her wings were willing, but she didn't mean to spook the Resurgence so early in the morning.

Earth, the way the Maker intended it, was beauty and love. Both children of the night and the day belonged here but not the faerie or their lycans. Whiteswoon was gone and so was Blackhunt, but seven other generals remained. Kara would hunt them down and kill them all. Bloods too, if they were intent on war. She'd found her home and she would protect it. She had a heart and would die for it. And that was what happiness was, wasn't it? It was elm trees, it was heavy fog, it was the smell of wet earth and the morning dew, the scent of burning wood, and the rustle of the forest soil underneath her tires—and most of all, it was loving someone enough to kill for them, and be loved in return.

From the Author

Thank you, as always, for reading. The story lives not when I write, but when you read.

A special thanks to Jeri and Shelby for their invaluable feedback, and to my editor, Sheryl Lee, who is always too kind.

I hope you enjoyed the story of Kara and Lucien. Even though this is a stand-alone piece, I have other series that you might be interested in. My writing includes foul language, dark magic, a high body count, and adult scenes. If that's your cup of tea, please visit my website and consider signing up for my newsletter at:

Brienfeathers.com

You can also explore my other series on my site, or you'll find an 'Also By' page following this one.

Love and light,

B. Feathers

Also by Brien Feathers

The **Sun War Trilogy** is a dark fantasy series inspired by Slavic folklore. It is set during the Bolshevik Revolution, where the utilitarian state clashes with the tsarists, depicted as a court of magic within the story.

Warlock of Muscovy, Book 1

Dragon of Akari, Book 2

Alchemist of the Machines, Book 3

The **Light of Adua** dark fantasy series is set in modern-day New Orleans, where vampires wielding magic are engaged in a war against an ancient realm.

Silver to the Heart, Book 1

Prophecy for the Warlord, Book 2

Vanity of the Whisperer, Book 3

Blood for the Snow, Book 4

Loss for the Prince, Book 5

Death of the Guardian, Book 6

War for the Realm, Book 7

www.ingramcontent.com/pod-product-compliance
Lightning Source LLC
Chambersburg PA
CBHW020328160726
47992CB00004B/1752